PRESSED

A Kurt Vetter and Amanda Carter Thriller

The Hunt is on...

WILLIAM ESMONT

Book Two of the Reluctant Hero Series

Print edition January 2012
ISBN 978-1468189223

www.williamesmont.com

Susan,
I hope you enjoy
the story!
– Bill E.

ACKNOWLEDGMENTS

They say it takes a village to raise a child. I believe the same maxim applies to writing a novel. For the most part, the ideas are already in my head. The act of transforming them into what you are about to read, however, requires a complex orchestration of people and resources beyond anything I ever could have imagined when I first put pen to paper. My wife is the closest person to this process—the one who listens patiently as I ramble about my characters and plot threads. She's the one who puts up with my moodiness and encourages me to keep pushing at this crazy endeavor. Thank you, Robin! Next up are my creative partners, Lynn O'Dell, who edits my raw stories, and Glendon Haddix, who turns my cheesy blurbs into eye-catching covers. I would be lost without your assistance. Finally, I'd like to acknowledge my beta readers. Beta readers are the brave souls who volunteer to hunt down problems in my manuscript before you, the reader, encounter them. The gift of their time puts me forever in their debt. I'd like to thank my parents, Tony and Gretchen, Mark Jaggers, Don Query, Chris Weicht, Dan Moore, U.S. Army Major Daniel Morris, Becky Smith, and Chris Merhige for their input. Your suggestions have made this a stronger book, and a piece of each of you will live forever in this story.

OTHER BOOKS BY WILLIAM ESMONT

Espionage Thriller:

The Patriot Paradox (The Reluctant Hero, Book One)

Pressed (The Reluctant Hero, Book Two)

Horror:

Fire: Elements of the Undead Book One

Air: An Elements of the Undead Novelette

Bio-Thriller:

Self Arrest

ONE

Washington, DC
The South Lawn of the White House

THE SLIDING DOOR OF THE VH-60N White Hawk was barely closed when Marine One tore free from the ground, its rotors clawing at the dense air blanketing the capital. The twin T701C "Charlie" turbo-shafts screamed like banshees as the pilot pulled in an armload of collective in a determined effort to evacuate the President in the most direct manner possible.

"Go! Go! Go!" the Marine in the copilot seat screamed, his voice barely audible over the shriek of the engine.

Kurt Vetter leaned around the Secret Service agent seated to his right and watched the lights of the capital recede. The lights vanished for an instant, and he realized the chopper was crossing over the Potomac and into Northern Virginia. The lights reappeared. He wasn't sure, but it seemed as if the pilot was tracking the George Washington Parkway, heading northwest.

"Sir?" the Secret Service agent shouted over the roar of the rotors. "Please move away from the window."

Kurt stared into the man's eyes, trying to read his intent. The agent tossed his head in the direction of Kurt's seat. Kurt moved.

Nothing in Kurt's life could have prepared him for the events of the past week. Ten minutes earlier, he had stood before the President of the United States, about to receive the Presidential Medal of Freedom for his part in disrupting a rogue CIA plot to destroy Moscow. Before the President had been able to finish his speech, the Secret Service burst into the room with news of a nuclear attack on Norfolk, Virginia. He had immediately been engulfed in a phalanx of security personnel with one overriding goal: remove the President from the capital. The evacuation was frantic, yet controlled, no doubt one of hundreds of contingency plans designed to preserve the government in the event of a catastrophic attack on American soil.

The President sat directly across from Kurt, his attention focused on a bulky radio headset. He seemed to have aged ten years in the past few minutes. His normally ruddy complexion had turned an ashen shade of gray, and his mouth was bent into a vicious frown. His expression vacillated between anger and bewilderment as he struggled to comprehend the possibility of a nuclear attack on his watch.

The helicopter banked hard to the right, pitching Kurt across the rich leather bench seat and tossing him into his neighbor. "Sorry," he yelled, as he extricated himself. In the hurry to board, he had forgotten to fasten his safety belt.

"Don't worry about it," Amanda Carter shouted back. She held out a buckle. *His* buckle. Kurt saw that she was already strapped in.

Their eyes met, and he caught a glint of amused sympathy in her expression before she replaced it with a hard smile.

Kurt took the buckle and fastened his own harness, giving it a good tug to make sure it was tight.

Ever since his brother Mike, a disgruntled member of the corrupt CIA cell, had passed Kurt details about the scheme and directed him to seek Amanda in London, Kurt's life had been a series of near-misses, a barrage of cloak-and-dagger activities far exceeding the scope of his meager CIA analyst training. He had been trying to play catch-up ever since.

Amanda, he had discovered, was well-versed in the world of covert operations. In an attempt to take Mike's information to the authorities, she and Kurt had embarked on a breakneck journey culminating in a shootout with a group of rebels in an abandoned warehouse in Moscow. Kurt and Amanda had taken advantage of the element of surprise, but the confrontation had quickly fallen apart due to the sheer number of adversaries. Only the eleventh-hour arrival of a team of Russian soldiers, tipped off by the President himself, had helped them prevent the destruction of the Russian Federation.

He leaned close to her ear, so he wouldn't have to yell. "What do you think is going on?"

Amanda gestured at the President and gave an exaggerated shrug, as if to say *I don't know.*

Kurt shifted his attention to the Secret Service agent sitting beside the President. In her mid-forties, with the lean body of a long-time marathoner and eyes that never seemed to rest, she seemed to be in charge of the security procedures. He waved to get her attention. Her response was quick: a shake of the head and a finger to her lips.

Frustrated, Kurt turned to the only other occupant of the passenger compartment, the National Security Advisor. Dominic Velasquez wore a headset, and he was also deep in conversation. His fingers furiously swiped and stabbed at the tablet computer in his lap as he took notes. He looked almost as frustrated as the President.

Seated behind the President and his party, in minimalist jump seats, were two steely-eyed Marines in full Battle Dress Uniforms, or BDUs. They watched Kurt intently, as if he were some sort of novel creature, an intruder in their carefully controlled environment.

He gave up on getting any answers. He decided to try to get comfortable. He still didn't know where they were headed or how long they would be in the air. He was exhausted and wanted nothing more than to go home, crack open a beer, collapse onto his couch, and forget everything that had happened in the past several weeks.

It had all started with a phone call from his mother. His brother Mike was dead, a victim of what had appeared at first to be a random shooting. Kurt had been in Peru at the time, mired in a self-imposed exile, trying to come to grips with the deaths of his wife and daughter several months prior. After the call, Kurt had raced back to the States, only to receive a package from his dead brother. Inside, he found a memory card overflowing with classified data and instructions to seek Amanda in London. From that point on, his life had been a nauseating blur. Deciphering the data and understanding the full scope of the plot became his reason for existence, his personal mission, yet a task he was ill-equipped to handle alone. Out of necessity, Amanda had become his other half.

Kurt tried to guess their distance from Norfolk, the

source of the attack. He peered out the port window, to the south, and scanned the moonless night sky for the telltale signs of an explosion.

"What are you doing?" Amanda asked.

Kurt mimed an explosion with his hands.

She shook her head. "We're too far away."

He didn't believe her. There should at least be some trace, a glow on the horizon perhaps, some sign of the destruction.

A hand tapped his knee. Kurt looked down. It was Dominic, trying to get his attention, holding his hands over his ears and then pointing at the floor. Kurt stared at him, confused for a long moment, until he realized what the National Security Advisor was trying to say. *Headset. Under the seat.* Kurt leaned forward and groped around until his hand brushed something dangling from a hook. Amanda followed suit. Slipping the headset over his ears, Kurt was pleasantly surprised to discover that it drowned out most of the rotor noise, and he could hear again.

"Thanks," Dominic said. "The President wants you in on this call."

"Uh, sure." Kurt adjusted his boom microphone.

"Hello, Kurt. Amanda." President Cooper still wore a frown.

"Mr. President," Kurt replied, unsure what was expected of him. He detected a similar hint of uncertainty in Amanda's voice as she echoed his greeting.

The President pressed on. "Something strange is going on, something unprecedented. I have Captain Rick Pettibone on the line, as well as most of my cabinet. Captain Pettibone is currently sitting on the bridge of the aircraft carrier George H. W. Bush in Norfolk, Virginia."

Thought Kurt couldn't hear it, he felt the pitch of

the engines change. The helicopter banked hard to the right and began to climb again, pressing him deep into his seat.

"But I thought..." Amanda sputtered.

The President gave her a sharp look. "Captain Pettibone, could you please repeat your situation report?"

An older man's voice laced with traces of a deep southern accent came on line. "Yes, sir, Mister President. Skies are clear. Visibility extends four to five miles. Winds are out of the southwest at five knots. No sign of any explosion."

"Thank you, Captain," the President said. "Please stand by."

"Yes, sir."

The President directed his gaze to Kurt. Kurt sensed all eyes on him. Not knowing what else to say, and not sure why the President was looking to him, he blurted the first thing that came to mind. "Could it be a false alarm?"

A female voice chimed in. "This is June Ames at Defense. That's highly unlikely. The systems involved in this type of alert are heavily encrypted and have multiple human beings in the loop to guard against that sort of thing."

Kurt stole a glance at Amanda. She appeared lost in thought, her chin cupped in her hand, and her eyes closed.

The phone beeped. "Mr. President, this is Charlie Howell at NSA. I'd like to bring Darlene Foster into the call."

The President tilted his head. "Sure, Charlie."

Kurt exhaled, relieved the spotlight had shifted away from him. He had never been a fast thinker, preferring to mull over a problem before voicing his opinions. That was why he had ended up on the analytical side of the CIA, rather than in operations like his brother.

"This is, uh, Darlene Foster," a new voice said. She sounded young, not quite sure of herself.

"Go ahead, Ms. Foster," the President said.

"Thanks. When the Strategic Early Warning System detects a threat, one of the first things that occurs is a flash backup of the Federal information technology infrastructure, to create a snapshot of everything in case it is—"

"Destroyed?" the President interjected.

"Yes. Destroyed. We've been doing this since around 2005. Prior to then, we didn't have the technology or the bandwidth to capture everything."

"I think I'm following you."

"Good. Don't hesitate to stop me if I get too technical. As I was saying, we conduct a backup, piping a copy of the entire Federal communications stream to several datacenters around the country. Fort Meade and Denver, for instance. This all happens without any human intervention."

"And how long does this take?"

"Minutes," Darlene replied.

"And you grab everything?" Dominic asked, cutting in.

"Yes. The process is always running behind the scenes; it's just a matter of making it a higher priority activity, which brings me to my next point. A small cluster of servers in the Pentagon, part of the SEWS, or Strategic Early Warning System, rejected the backup command. This doesn't happen. At least, it hasn't happened until today. The failure triggered a battery of diagnostic processes responsible for ensuring the health of the system. The diagnostic programs search for all sorts of things—excessive bandwidth utilization, processor load, rogue programs, even viruses—anything with the potential to cause a system failure..."

"A hacker," Amanda whispered when Darlene paused to catch her breath.

"One moment," the President said, holding up a finger. "What was that, Ms. Carter?"

"A hacker. Someone probing the SEWS communications infrastructure—"

Darlene cleared her throat. "That was my thought exactly. Someone hacked the system. How they did it, I have no idea. Why? Well, that's the fifty million dollar question."

The President's face turned red, and he clenched his fists. "God dammit! This system is tied to our nuclear weapons, for Christ's sake." He glared at the agent beside him.

After an uncomfortable silence, June Ames spoke up again, her voice thin and reedy. "I assure you, Mr. President, we'll get to the bottom of this. There are only so many people who have this type of access."

The President closed his eyes and tilted his head back, apparently deep in thought. Kurt held his breath and waited for the hammer to drop.

The President opened his eyes and ordered, "Turn us around. We're going back to DC."

"Sir," the agent said. "We can't do that. Not yet."

The President glared at her. "And why not?"

"We have protocols to follow. We're going to Mount Weather until we can ensure the security situation has stabilized."

Kurt observed the exchange with a growing sense of dread. He wasn't certain he would ever get home.

TWO

Silver Spring, Maryland

GREG MILLER CHANGED THE CHANNEL from CNN to MSNBC to FOX and then back to CNN. The story was the same everywhere. Washington D.C. was in a state of chaos unlike any seen since 9/11. Forty minutes earlier, according to the pretty young CNN commentator, the White House had gone on high alert. All non-essential personnel, the press included, had been escorted from the building and told to return to their bureaus and await further instruction. A few minutes later, the Presidential helicopter roared in low over the treetops and touched down on the West Lawn. According to an unnamed source, the President and his National Security Advisor, along with several unnamed civilians, had dashed from the building, surrounded by a full coterie of Secret Service agents. They had all piled into the helicopter and roared away, heading northwest.

Greg couldn't tear his attention from the screen. His stomach roiled, a not-so-subtle protest of the predicament in which he found himself.

His thoughts jumped back two years, to the annual Advanced Defense Technology conference in New York City, where he had first met the mysterious Russian man he knew only as Vasily. On the morning of the first day of the conference, at breakfast, the Russian had pulled up a chair beside Greg and introduced himself. He claimed to be the business development manager for a small European firm specializing in ceramics. Greg had never heard of the company before, but didn't think much of it at the time, as his specialty was self-healing computer networks, an entirely different industry. At first, Greg had viewed Vasily as a mere nuisance, one of the countless corporate sycophants who spent their lives trolling the halls of industry events in search of intelligence on their competitors' activities. That all changed, however, as their conversation drifted into details of Greg's work. It had seemed so natural at the time. In hindsight, he wasn't able to pinpoint what had made him speak so freely. He supposed it was the subtle encouragement Vasily had provided, the head nods, the flattering comments about his work, maybe even the way Vasily had refilled Greg's coffee cup before Greg even realized he needed more. Whatever it was, it had worked, and he had opened up far more than he had intended. Once breakfast was over and Vasily was gone, Greg tried his best to convince himself he hadn't revealed anything confidential, that the conversation was merely a friendly exchange between two industry professionals. Still, he couldn't shake the novelty of speaking with someone who appeared to be genuinely interested in his work, and deep down, he wished he had had more time to chat.

He didn't see Vasily for the next four days and had almost forgotten about their exchange until a coffee break on the afternoon of the final day. As the barista handed him his tall double-shot Americano, he sensed a presence behind him. Turning, he found Vasily, only a few feet away, grinning at him.

Greg moved away from the coffee cart and blew on his drink. "Hello again."

Vasily quickly closed the distance between them. "Hello, Mr. Miller. I trust you have had a productive conference."

"I have. It's been quite a week." That was a gross exaggeration, of course. The truth was, he had found only one session to be worth his attendance, and even the information he had learned there could have been gathered from the internet. Still, it had been a good excuse to get out of D.C. for a few days.

"Very good," Vasily said, his gaze flicking past Greg's shoulders. "I was hoping to speak with you one more time before you left. If you have a moment—"

Greg couldn't put his finger on it, but something in Vasily's gaze, the way his eyes never seemed to stop moving, put him on alert. His earlier feelings of discomfort with the Russian's questions came rushing back, and he felt the hairs on the back of his neck stand up. It was no coincidence Vasily had sought him out, he realized with a startling clarity.

"I'm sorry," Greg said, casting about for some excuse to get away before he said something else he shouldn't. "I have to meet some people in a few minutes."

Disappointment—or was it annoyance?—flashed across Vasily's face, but the emotion was gone in an instant, replaced with an understanding smile. "That is too bad." Vasily held out his hand, and from within the folds of his palm, Greg glimpsed the edges of a business card. "Please, do not hesitate to call me if you change your mind, if you wish to talk more. I enjoyed our discussion, and who knows? We may be able to help each other in the future..."

Acting on autopilot, Greg extended his hand and shook with the Russian. When Vasily pulled away, the sharp edges of a stiff business card remained in Greg's palm, a tactile symbol of the invisible line he had just crossed. Without looking at it, Greg put his hand in his pocket and deposited the card.

"Uh. Okay. It was nice meeting you."

"Enjoy the rest of the conference."

"I will. You too," Greg said.

With a quick nod, Vasily turned and melted into the crowd.

Greg took a deep breath and made his way to an unoccupied lounge chair. He pulled the business card out of his pocket and stared at it. It was blank except for a Manhattan phone number. For a moment, he considered leaving the card on the arm of the chair and walking away from what looked and felt like an improper contact. At the last moment, he changed his mind and returned the card to his pocket. *Just in case.*

The following Monday, when he returned to his office, Greg submitted a suspicious contact report, documenting everything he could recall about the incident. He disclosed the conversation they had had over breakfast, the way Vasily had probed him. He left nothing out. Except the card. For reasons he still didn't quite understand, he kept that for himself. Taped to the underside of the desk in his study, it was his little secret, his way of retaining a small sliver of privacy in a world where privacy had become a dirty word.

Within a week of returning from the conference, Greg's life had returned to normal. He spent the next year and a half focusing on his work, not giving a single moment's thought to Vasily and their meeting in New York until six months ago, in the dead of winter, when he had lost his job at the Synax Corporation. It wasn't his fault his job went away, not by a long shot. His contract was the unfortunate victim of an industry-wide round of budget cuts, a routine occurrence in Washington, but for the first time, Greg had been the one left holding the bag. At first, he had viewed the unexpected break as an opportunity, a time to catch up on his reading, maybe even do a little traveling. But the job market continued to deteriorate. Layoffs mounted. There was no more work. Every morning, he sent out fresh copies of his resume. He worked Facebook, LinkedIn, and Twitter, all to no avail. The defense industry held its breath, waiting to see which way the federal government lurched next. Before long, his savings had been exhausted, but not before the balloon payment on his four-bedroom house came due. Greg had needed cash, and he needed it fast.

Desperate to avoid losing his home, he had done the unthinkable. He had called Vasily.

A woman picked up on the second ring. Greg couldn't detect an accent, but that didn't mean anything. "I'm looking for Vasily."

The woman covered the phone and yelled something Greg couldn't decipher. A moment later, Vasily came on the line.

"Yes?"

Greg sucked in his breath. "We met in New York. A few years ago. I have your card..."

He didn't want to use his name. He wasn't ready to cross that line.

After a pause, Vasily said, "It is good to hear from you."

Greg couldn't help but notice Vasily hadn't used his name either. Whether the omission had been intentional or not, he couldn't tell.

"I assume you are interested in my proposal?"

Greg chewed his lip and shuffled his feet. "I am."

Vasily chuckled, low and throaty. "Are you sure?"

Anxiety gripped Greg as he envisioned a counterespionage sting unfolding around him. He pushed back his fear, telling himself it had been too long, that if he were being tested, his watchers would have long ago abandoned their hunt.

"I'm sure."

"Do you have a pen?"

"Hold on." He pulled a ballpoint from his jacket pocket. "Yes."

"Good. This is the last time we will speak. Go to this address."

Greg scribbled the address on the back of his hand. "Got it."

"Tell the man behind the counter you need to speak to someone about a loan."

Greg stared at the ink drying on his hand. "Okay. Then what—"

The line went dead.

Greg went to the address the next afternoon. It turned out to be a small convenience store in Georgetown, wedged between a high-end cigar store and a nail salon.

"Camel Blues," he said as he approached the register.

The man at the counter appeared to be in his mid-fifties. Something in the way his gray eyes flitted between Greg and the dense bank of security cameras over the counter gave Greg the impression the man was used to looking over his shoulder. Butterflies ricocheted around Greg's stomach. He cleared his throat.

"I feel stupid for asking this, and please don't be offended... but..." He looked around once again to make sure he was alone. “Do you know anyone who could loan me some money? I have a bit of an emergency...”

The cashier squinted at him and said nothing for a moment. He slid a pack of cigarettes across the counter. “Matches?”

Greg was confused. He decided to try again, in case the man hadn’t heard him. “I’m sorry. Maybe I didn’t make myself clear. Vasily said—”

The cashier scratched his chin. Inscrutable. “I’m sorry.”

Greg scooped up the cigarettes and stuffed them in his pocket. He zipped his coat to his collar. “I’m sorry to have bothered you.”

“No problem.” The cashier took a seat on the stool behind the register and picked up his mobile phone. He tapped the screen a few times, appearing to forget about Greg.

Greg turned for the door, steeling himself for the blast of arctic air waiting outside.

“Mister?” the cashier said.

Greg turned.

The man held up his phone. A sly smile creased his face. “Vasily, you said?”

Greg pulled the door closed. “Uh huh.”

The cashier pushed a button on the top of the register, and several inches of purple-lined paper curled out with a low mechanical hum. He tore off the paper, scribbled on it, then folded it in half. He slid the paper across the counter to Greg. “Call this number.”

Greg took the paper and opened it. *Viktor. 202-421-7764. DC.* “Thanks.” He slipped the paper into his jeans pocket and left the store. He didn’t notice the cold on the way back to his car.

The next steps were nothing like what he had expected. He met Viktor Durov in a Starbucks in

Dupont circle, where they made their deal over a pair of skinny caramel macchiatos and low-fat banana nut muffins. A day later, Greg's mortgage was paid off, his house secure.

Two days later, he received his first assignment—an encrypted zip file of partially-functioning computer code. The file contained endless pages of government warnings and top-secret classification markings. Viktor's instructions were simple.

Make it work. You have one month.

The bundle contained a mishmash of incomplete software. The most intriguing was a peer-to-peer worm, a piece of code that would propagate itself through the U. S. Strategic Early Warning System, attaching itself to the myriad of systems responsible for detecting and analyzing nuclear attacks on the United States. What the worm did, Greg was never able to discern. He had a nagging suspicion it was more complex than it appeared. By that point, though, he was committed. He had already violated every oath he had ever taken by contacting Vasily. There was no going back. Greg pressed on, determined to finish his assignment and get on with his life, whatever was left of it.

He heard nothing from Viktor for almost two weeks after he submitted his final delivery. Then, early in the morning on the first warm day in April, he received an encrypted instant message from Viktor notifying him his work had been accepted and that he was a free man. In addition, fifty-thousand dollars appeared in his bank account, an unexpected and very welcome gesture of good will.

For a few months, Greg was almost able forget what he had done, to believe he was free, that it was all a bad dream. Until ten days ago...

A young woman close to his own age had appeared

on his doorstep carrying a pair of powerful laptops and wearing a grim, tired expression.

The code had only been the beginning.

Greg worked with the woman for the next forty-eight hours, configuring the same software he had modified, and teaching her how to install it in an operational environment. The woman barely said a word the entire time, dodging Greg's attempts to discover her identity and the extent of her relationship with Viktor. By the time they finished, she was able to install and configure the software on her own. She vanished while Greg slept on his couch, taking with her both laptops and all traces of their work together.

That was a little over a week ago.

Turning off the television, Greg struggled to his feet. His hands shook uncontrollably, and his knees felt as though they were full of ball bearings. Visions of blue-jacketed FBI agents crashing through his front door rooted him in place, sending crippling waves of ice-cold fear coursing through his body. Putting his hand to his mouth, he tried to choke back the contents of his stomach, but failed as it finally won the battle.

THREE

Georgetown, Washington, DC

VIKTOR DUROV MUTED THE TELEVISION above the bar. He finished the last of his beer and pushed his glass across the varnished wood toward the bartender, holding up an open palm to cut the man off when he moved to refill it. He stubbed out his cigarette in an empty ashtray, then picked up his mobile phone and stepped away from the bar.

There was a soft click on the line after the second ring, and then the tone changed, becoming more insistent as the call was routed to an international exchange. A man answered. "Da?" *Yes?*

Viktor cleared his throat. "Are you watching?"

The man switched to heavily accented English. "Yes. It is good."

Viktor smiled. "Good" was an understatement. It was perfect.

He heard the clatter of fingers on a keyboard. He waited, turning so he could see the television again. On the screen, a middle-aged man with a microphone stood in front of the White House, gesturing at a group of dour-faced Marines standing guard. A banner scrolled across the bottom of the screen, repeating what Viktor already knew.

The white house has been evacuated. Washington, D.C. is under temporary military control.

"And your employees?" the man on the phone said, his voice revealing no hint of emotion.

Viktor ran his fingers through his thin hair. "Severance packages have been arranged." Viktor imagined Greg Miller's and Melody Jackson's expressions when they next met. His smile twisted into a sneer as he pictured putting a gun to each of their heads and pulling the trigger. "It's under control."

A pause. "Good."

Viktor licked his lips. He wanted another beer. Talking to Alexander Yolkin never failed to make him want to drink.

"Keep me posted," the man on the phone said, and then ended the call abruptly.

Viktor glanced at the screen to verify the connection had been severed. He tucked his phone into the front pocket of his pants. Turning, he swaggered back to the bar. "Tully!"

The bartender, a gaunt man with a receding hairline and a thick salt-and-pepper mustache, grabbed a fresh glass from the rack over the bar.

Viktor held up a finger. "Just a second..." He turned to face the room. The bar was half full, maybe twenty people. "Drinks are on me!" he bellowed. A smattering of applause erupted from the patrons. Viktor turned back to Tully and motioned for him to continue.

By all accounts, what he had just accomplished would go down in the history books of Russian intelligence. The network intrusion wasn't just a breach of security in one of the most secure environments in the world. No, breaking into the US Early Warning system was the fulfillment of a longstanding dream of the reconstituted Russian intelligence services, or GRU, to prove they were once again technical and intelligence equals of their American counterparts, able to operate with impunity on foreign soil.

Viktor was one of the first of a new generation of Russian spies. Born in New Jersey to Russian immigrants and raised in the suburbs of Washington, D.C., he enjoyed the freedoms inherent in citizenship, yet his allegiance lay firmly in the clutches of the country of his ancestors. Raised as a typical American boy, he played little league and soccer, attended a modest public school in his suburban neighborhood, and even went to Disney World for his tenth birthday.

It wasn't until his seventeenth year that his destiny became apparent. He had been on vacation in Russia with his father, visiting his cousins and seeing his motherland for the first time. After dinner on the second day of the trip, his father made an unexpected comment about how much he missed the old Russia, about how he wished Viktor could have seen it before the fall. That was the first time Viktor had heard his father speak of Russia in such a way, the old man's voice full of an unrepentant nostalgia, an aching, almost crippling wistfulness.

"Sure, Dad," Viktor said, taking a sip of his Coca-Cola.

"What if…" His father turned to face him. "What if we could make it so again? Bring back the old Russia?" His father's eyes bored into him, freezing him in place.

Viktor squirmed. He didn't know how to respond. He had always assumed his parents had left Russia for a better life, to escape the poverty, the crime, and the lawlessness. To be free.

It turned out he had been living a lie since before he could walk. Viktor recoiled in disgust as his father revealed the plan hatched long ago inside the Kremlin, in the last desperate days of the Soviet Union, when the leadership had finally accepted the imminent dissolution of their country. He planned to restore the Soviet Union, to reclaim greatness.

Viktor rejected his father outright, calling him a traitor, accusing him of using him and his mother to support a dead country. He stormed back to his hotel room, refusing to speak to his father. After a couple of days, his anger cooled, and they resumed their trip, talk of serving Russia conveniently ignored. They spent the month together touring the countryside, visiting family, and basking in the remnants of greatness.

Much to Viktor's surprise, he felt his attitudes changing; his perspective on the world and his place in it shifted with each passing day. By the end of the trip, he felt an unexpected and deep kinship with the people he had met and an overpowering sense of pride in his heritage, a visceral connection that suffused his entire being with a newfound sense of belonging.

Still, he said nothing to his father. He was afraid to revive the subject, unsure if he was prepared for the intensity he had seen in his father's eyes.

Viktor and his father, seated side-by-side in the second row of first class on an enormous Airbus A380, left Russia and returned to Washington. They barely spoke on the long journey across the North Atlantic, each ensconced in their own bubble of reflection. Viktor watched movies on his iPad while his father slept the sleep of a satisfied man.

As the plane sat on the tarmac at Dulles International Airport, Viktor made up his mind. He touched his father's forearm. "Dad?"

"Yes?" his father asked with a raised eyebrow. "What is it?"

The flight attendant pulled the lever on the cabin door, and the cabin pressure equalized with a *whoosh.*

Viktor looked around to make sure no one was listening. "About what you said back in Moscow..."

His father leaned forward. His eyes narrowed, a sly grin formed on his mouth. "Yes?"

Viktor swallowed. "I'll do it... what you talked about." In that moment, Viktor knew he had made the right decision. The tension that had weighed on his father since that first night vanished in an instant.

His father broke into a smile and patted Viktor's hand. "That's good, Viktor... that's good."

An American spy had been born.

Viktor wiped a tear from his eye. His father had died five years earlier, his body ravaged by a horrifically aggressive lung cancer. Viktor was an only child, the last in an illustrious line of Durovs, loyal servants of the Soviet state.

If only he could see me now, Viktor thought, a tear forming in the corner of his eye.

He downed his drink in one gulp and gathered his keys and phone. *Now to take care of my loose ends...*

FOUR

Outside of Cluj, Romania

MAGOMED GASANOV PUSHED HIS CHAIR back, stood, and surveyed his surroundings with a withering scowl. Despite spending the majority of his life in the former Soviet Union, he still couldn't understand the overriding obsession with pea green paint. The furniture, the walls, and even the cracked and peeling linoleum floors, were all tinted in the same unimaginative, soul-crushing shade. It depressed him.

Not that the color mattered. The facility, an ex-Soviet Army garrison tucked into the foothills of the Carpathian Mountains, was the perfect location for the task at hand. Magomed had rented it from the Romanian government, ostensibly to use as a training facility for a private security firm. He had to laugh at the irony of it. His men, hand-picked veterans of two vicious wars with the Russians, were better trained and more loyal than any private security firm could ever hope for.

Magomed took a deep breath and blew it out,

forcing himself to relax, to unwind. He knew it wouldn't do any good to let the situation cause him more stress. He had seen worse.

Progress had been slow since he and his men had pulled into the facility four days earlier. The high-voltage electrical lines feeding the compound had long ago fallen into disrepair, contrary to the promises of the leasing agent. The lack of reliable electricity had resulted in a two-day delay while two of his men salvaged several generators from the storage depot and procured a tanker truck of diesel fuel from the nearby town of Cluj, two hours to the southeast. Fortunately, the old Soviet generators, while antiquated, had been built to last. After a few hours of reconditioning, they roared to life on the first try.

Magomed strode from the room and set off down a long, dark hallway. He heard music emanating from a room at the far end of the hall, the tune muffled by the closed door. He picked up his pace. He knew they were close to achieving his goal. A day, maybe two, was what his old friend Pytor Melikov had promised, and Magomed was intent upon holding him to that promise if at all possible.

As he drew closer to the door, he detected the familiar dull rumble of the generators, the unfortunate soundtrack to his life on the run. The air was thick with the stench of diesel fuel, the vapors being drawn through the shoddily constructed building by the constant wind from the west. He had considered relocating the generators, but had changed his mind once Pytor explained the impact to the schedule if they were without power for an extended period.

Breathing through his mouth to avoid the stench, Magomed pushed into the room. The space had formerly been used as a vehicle maintenance shop. A row of unoccupied hydraulic lifts dominated a third of it, the dried grease on their pistons caking and cracking in great black sheets. In addition to the lifts, the room also contained a motley collection of ancient engine hoists, their over-engineered metal arms draped with chains and hooks waiting for vehicles that would never return. A line of olive-green metal workbenches, still stocked with tools, lined one wall. Garage doors covered the other wall, opening south to the former vehicle yard and the generators.

A mud-splattered black Mercedes Sprinter with Ukrainian license plates was parked in front of one of the closed garage doors.

In the center of the room, Magomed saw the object of his obsession—a five-foot-long dull-green cylinder, tapered to a point at one end. A nuclear warhead. The bomb, one of three MIRVs, or Multiple Independently targetable Reentry Vehicles, formerly attached to a decommissioned Soviet SS-20 ballistic missile, was his after a brilliant feat of deception in which he had outmaneuvered the Central Intelligence Agency.

He couldn't help but smile at his part in what was arguably one of the greatest bait-and-switch scams in history. The Americans had thought they were purchasing a fanatical martyr, a man who hated Moscow enough to destroy it and reignite the old conflict between East and West in one bold move. What they got instead was a dummy MIRV casing filled with low-level radioactive medical waste, not even enough for a dirty bomb. Once the switch was complete, Magomed and his crew had fled Moscow and driven southwest, crossing first into Belarus, and then Ukraine, before eventually entering Romanian territory, his new base of operations. He had chosen Romania for two reasons. First, it was economically stable. The country was still recovering from the chaos of the years before the new millennium, the period when the future was unknown and up for the taking. Also, it was politically stable after having finally made the transition to a true parliamentary democracy.

Pytor stood at a table beside the warhead. Somewhere in his mid-seventies, the former scientist with the Soviet Strategic Rocket Forces acted like a kid in a candy store. He knew the SS-20 inside and out, having been personally involved in the design of the first generation of the weapon. An unlit cigarette dangled from the corner of his mouth. American music, something from the sixties, blared from a battered black plastic radio perched on the edge of the workbench.

"Pytor!" Magomed bellowed.

The old man looked up in surprise. "Well, hello," Pytor answered in Russian. "Come to see your baby?"

Magomed nodded and looked past the old scientist. Components and tools were strewn across the workbench. An oblong lead box containing the warhead's plutonium pit sat in the center. A hand-held radiation detector lay beside the box, the needle resting at the low end of the green band. Safe.

Pytor waved a hand at the jumble of electronics. "I have all of the components prepared, but it is taking longer than expected to assemble everything." He turned and crossed the room to a stack of black plastic suitcases. He picked one up, and Magomed could tell they were heavier than they looked, probably lined with lead.

Struggling with the weight, Pytor hauled the case to the table. He swung it, building momentum, until he finally got enough to send it onto the table with a crash. A pile of tools skittered off the edge of the table, tumbling to the floor with a clatter.

Magomed cringed. The old man's cavalier manner around radioactive materials terrified him. The thought of being irradiated, of dying in this decrepit hellhole, was his worst nightmare.

Pytor placed his thumbs on the case's latches and popped them with a muted click. The lid sprung open, revealing an interior control panel festooned with a keypad, an LCD screen, and an empty compartment where the re-manufactured plutonium pit would reside.

"Looks good, no?" Pytor asked, admiring his own work.

Magomed ran his fingers over the numeric keypad, impressed with the craftsmanship. If Pytor was half as good at dividing the pit into multiple cores as he was at the electronics end of things, then he would indeed get what he was looking for—a portable nuclear device that he could sell on the black market. He pushed the case closed and lifted it to assess the weight. Not too bad, he thought, maybe fifteen or twenty kilos. The plutonium would add a little more, but the resulting bomb would still be portable.

"And the plutonium?" he asked, nodding at the lead box on the workbench.

Pytor's enthusiasm faded. "My equipment arrived this afternoon. Tomorrow, I will start dividing the pit."

Magomed set the case on the floor beside the workbench. He eyed the mostly unboxed crates of precision tools Pytor would use to manipulate the toxic metal. "Good. Do you think you'll have it complete before Friday?"

Pytor met his gaze. "I'll do my best."

Magomed didn't doubt him. Pytor was reliable to a fault; a true engineer, he was the consummate perfectionist, unable to walk away from a project until it was complete. The Friday deadline, only two days away, had been his idea to help spur Pytor on in his efforts. In reality, his first client meeting was not until the following week, but he wanted room for the inevitable problems that would arise.

The overhead lights flickered. Both men turned their attention toward the garage doors, outside of which the generators were installed. One of the generators coughed and sputtered, then backfired, before smoothing out and resuming its normal roar.

Magomed clenched his teeth. "I'd better go see about that."

Pytor took his seat and picked up a Phillips screwdriver. "Yes. Tomorrow, reliable power will become quite crucial."

Magomed knew all too well. The tolerances in the derivative plutonium cores were excessively precise. The smallest deviation could cut the yield of the device by seventy or eighty percent. The operation had to go exactly according to plan.

"Okay, then," Magomed said. "We'll talk later."

Pytor responded with a distracted grunt. He was already busy disassembling a detonator mechanism.

Magomed stood and watched for a moment, saying nothing. He divided his attention between the old man and the recalcitrant generator, waiting for a signal from either. Receiving none, he made for the door leading to the generators.

Only a few more problems to solve...

FIVE

Over Virginia

KURT FOLLOWED THE BACK AND forth between the President and his advisers with only half an ear as their conversation shifted into a discussion of crisis management and logistics. Their next stop was Mount Weather Emergency Operations Center, a twenty-five minute flight from Washington. Kurt had heard of the facility, but knew very little about it. Located in the northern Blue Ridge Mountains of Virginia, it was supposedly outfitted with enough electronics, communications gear, and supplies to allow the President to run the country for an extended period. Mount Weather hadn't been the Secret Service's first choice; they had wanted to get him onto Air Force One and into the air, high above any potential threats. President Cooper, however, had drawn the line at the rural bunker, declaring he wanted to be close to Washington so he could return as soon as possible.

From what Kurt could tell, it sounded as though the intrusion had triggered a far-reaching automated series of contingency plans, all designed to ensure the continuity of the government in the event of a major catastrophe. Some of the congressional leadership was also en route to Mount Weather, while others were being spirited to different locations around the country. The same applied to the judicial branch. The chief justice of the Supreme Court, currently in Miami on vacation, was being relocated to a military base in western Georgia.

How long those measures would remain in effect was unclear. The primary concern seemed to be that the security teams had no idea how deeply the hacker had penetrated. Initial reports indicated the damage was restricted to less than a dozen servers. However, no one was willing to give the all-clear until the military and NSA computer experts could complete a thorough review. And that took time.

The pitch of the helicopter engines changed, and Kurt's stomach lurched as the pilot initiated their descent. He looked out the window, searching for any sign of the facility, but saw nothing except dark forest and undulating hills.

Twenty seconds later, the helicopter settled on the tarmac with a soft bump. Kurt saw a flash of headlights moving toward them.

The Secret Service agent sitting next to him left his seat and hauled open the sliding door. The rotors still spun, so the open door caused the noise within the cabin to increase to a deafening shriek. The agent jumped out and dashed to the closer of two dark green Hummers waiting at the edge of the heliport.

The leader of the security detail leaped out, then she turned, motioning for the President to follow. The President had regained some of his composure during the trip. A gleam of confidence had replaced the look of defeat in his eyes, the same look he had so skillfully parlayed during his campaign two years earlier.

Dominic followed the president, ducking instinctively to avoid the rotors. The rotors had slowed to a crawl, making languid slicing sounds as it cut through the cool mountain air.

Kurt was next. He turned to Amanda. "This should be interesting."

She shot him a sardonic smile and unsnapped her safety harness.

Kurt stood, hunched over, and leaped from the helicopter, landing on the hard concrete with a bone-jarring thump. Amanda touched down beside him, graceful as a cat.

The Marine guards piled out of the helicopter behind them. "Ma'am. Sir. Please come with us," the taller of the two Marines instructed.

"But..." Kurt protested, gesturing at the President's group.

Amanda touched her hand to his lower back, sending a chill up his spine. The tension between them had been mounting since their flight across Europe, amplified and magnified by the constant threat of death from an assassin's bullet. For the first time since his wife had died, Kurt felt attracted to another woman, and he suspected Amanda felt the same about him. He thought the time was coming when they would be forced to confront their feelings for each other, to acknowledge what neither had been able to vocalize.

"Don't worry. We'll catch up with them," she said. Her hand fell away.

The President's group strode toward the other Humvee. The President and Dominic had mobile phones pressed to their ears, both men enmeshed in the throes of crisis management.

The Marines waited patiently, their weapons held

at-arms, ready to act on a moment's notice. Their eyes scanned their surroundings continuously, searching for threats from all directions.

Kurt watched, wracked by feelings of impotence, as the doors of the presidential Humvee slammed shut, and the vehicle roared into the night.

Kurt signaled the taller Marine with a nod. "Okay. We're all yours." They piled into the second Humvee and set off in the opposite direction from the President.

Kurt couldn't shake the feeling that his life was no longer his own.

~ * * * ~

Amanda took a deep breath and watched Kurt from her perch on the rock-hard rear seat of the Humvee. The exhaustion on his face mirrored exactly how she felt. She thought back to their time together in the White House, before the evacuation. Kurt had taken her hand and squeezed it. In that instant, she had felt something pass between them, some understanding that their bond might be deeper than it appeared from the outside. Kurt's hand was only inches from hers, splayed on the seat to balance himself.

Amanda chewed on her lip, debating her next move. Despite her fatigue, she felt alive, coursing with raw energy, hyper-aware of her surroundings and of the man sitting beside her. She didn't need the complication, though. Her mere presence on American soil carried a whole host of problems that thankfully hadn't yet surfaced. But when they did, she knew her life would become infinitely more complicated. Her past stalked her, and she had a bad feeling it was about to pounce.

With superhuman effort, she willed her hand loose

from its grip on her bag. Slow at first, and then faster as she shed her bonds of propriety, she slid it across to Kurt's until they touched. She squeezed. His hand stiffened, then relaxed. His palm turned to meet hers.

Their eyes met, and for the first time in as long as she could remember, Amanda felt a sense of calm.

SIX

Moscow, Russia
Main Intelligence Directorate (GRU) Headquarters

ALEXANDER YOLKIN RAISED HIS TEACUP to his nose and inhaled, savoring the complex blend of aromas wafting forth. He took a sip, and with a satisfied sigh, returned the heavy porcelain mug to its home beside his keyboard. Then he turned his attention to his screen. As the director of Nuclear Technology for the Russian Foreign Intelligence Service (SVR), he was responsible for locating and retrieving any rogue nuclear material that might pose a security threat to the Russian Federation. Alexander was well aware the success of his mission could launch his career into the stratosphere, making it the crowning achievement in his forty years of service. He was also painfully cognizant of the price of failure. He scratched at an old acne scar on his jaw and frowned. At sixty-one years old and after having spent his entire career with the SVR, he had faced a real challenge for the first time in which he wasn't confident of the outcome.

That worried him.

Following the collapse of the Soviet regime, the Russian government had launched a sweeping campaign to collect and inventory all radioactive materials not under their control. At the time, no one in power truly appreciated the scope of the task at hand. The Soviet Union had been an early and enthusiastic adopter of atomic technologies, from city-busting thermonuclear weapons all the way down to the myriad nuclear-powered lighthouses and autonomous weather stations dotting the polar regions of their sprawling empire. With the newly opened borders and the entirety of Eastern Europe clamoring for self-rule, retrieving all of that material before it vanished into the black market was a herculean task, far beyond the abilities of any one man. Yet Alexander and his team had prevailed, doggedly collecting the radioactive detritus and bringing it back under control of the central authority. Each successive victory brought him more power and autonomy, solidifying his position within the SVR, and to a degree, within the Russian elite. He soon controlled a sprawling empire of his own, directing multiple teams of SVR agents around the globe, dabbling in all manner of issues related to nuclear material, and sometimes even venturing into the realm of raw espionage.

The past several hours had passed in a blur as Alexander tracked the events unfolding in Washington. In hindsight, it had only been a matter of extraordinary timing and good fortune that he had activated Viktor Durov when he had. When first approached with the idea by his superiors, he had pushed back, arguing that bringing the American operative on-line was an extravagant act of speculation. But in the end, his superiors had forced the issue. They wanted to flex their muscles, to demonstrate Russia once again had the capability to reach across the Atlantic and touch their historic adversary, and they wanted Alexander to lead the charge. Everyone involved understood that the plan to probe the American security infrastructure with a phantom nuclear attack carried a high level of political and economic risk for the Russian Federation, yet, to Alexander's amazement, someone far above his pay grade had decreed the risk acceptable.

It wasn't the first time Alexander had been tasked with running a high-profile foreign espionage operation, but it was by far the most risky. At the same time, he was also in charge of tracking down the people responsible for the dirty bomb that had nearly detonated in Moscow several weeks earlier. The two events were inextricably linked. With the greater United States intelligence apparatus in disarray and their CIA effectively neutered by their part in the Moscow bomb scandal, it was the moment for which he had been waiting. Without hesitation, he had ordered Viktor Durov to proceed.

As far as he could tell from the media coverage, the operation was proceeding as planned. Washington had been evacuated, the President moved to an undisclosed location. According to his counterparts in the Russian military, there were no obvious signs of American nuclear force mobilizations. He surmised that they had determined the warning was a software glitch and were focusing more on the technology implications, just as he had hoped.

Alexandar took another sip of his tea, then picked up his phone. "Please get me the President," he told his assistant. He had a status report he was happy to deliver.

SEVEN

Mount Weather, Virginia

CIVILIAN QUARTERS AT MOUNT WEATHER were situated two hundred feet below the surface, encased in a hardened bunker designed to withstand all but the most extreme nuclear blasts. Each room measured eight by ten feet, with a government-issue steel-framed bed, a gray wooden dresser, and a utilitarian nightstand. A simple steel toilet and sink crowned by an unbreakable stainless steel mirror rounded out the amenities. Kurt couldn't help but think of a prison cell.

Upon landing at the facility, he and Amanda had been whisked underground by their Marine escorts, photographed, given limited-access plastic identity badges, and then deposited in the civilian quarters on the fifth sub-level. With nothing else to do but wait, they decided to find the mess hall and grab a bite to eat. Neither had eaten since early in the day, and with all of the excitement of meeting the President and their sudden exodus from Washington, they had burned through any last vestiges of energy.

They followed the signs on the walls to the mess hall, passing numerous soldiers and other civilians along the way. Everyone appeared busy, striding through the halls with eyes glued to folders and tablet computers or speaking on mobile phones. Kurt wondered how they worked underground until Amanda pointed out the small round repeaters embedded in the ceiling—a private underground cellular phone network, similar to those used in the metro subway tunnels around Washington.

Reaching the cafeteria, they got in line, each taking a light brown, rectangular plastic tray from a spring-loaded rack. Amanda went first, loading up on salad, but going easy on the dressing. Kurt had no such reservations. He took two slices of pepperoni pizza and an enormous wedge of chocolate cake topped with a mountain of firm whipped cream.

"That'll kill you, you know," Amanda commented with a smirk as he shifted his plates around to make room for his desert.

"This is the least of my worries at the moment." He tried to decide if wanted some apple pie as well. *Not yet.*

"Good point." Amanda took a bowl of tapioca pudding and nestled it beside the salad on her tray.

At the end of the line, Kurt reached for his wallet.

The attendant waved his money away. "That's not necessary, Mr. Vetter," she said, eying the badge dangling from his shirt pocket.

Kurt shrugged and stuffed his money back into his wallet. "Uh, okay."

The attendant held out her hand. "I do need to scan your badges, though."

Kurt and Amanda unclipped their badges and handed them over. The attendant ran them under a laser scanner, generating a soft beep for each badge.

Just like shopping at Lowe's, Kurt thought, as he clipped his badge back onto his shirt.

They took their trays and crossed the room to a quiet table in the far corner, well out of the earshot of other diners.

"So?" Amanda asked. "What do you think of all of this?"

Kurt peeled a pepperoni from one of his slices and popped it into his mouth. "It's smaller than I thought it would be."

Amanda smiled and stabbed her fork into her salad, spearing a load of lettuce and spinach. "Smaller, huh? That's not really what I was talking about, you know?"

"Yeah. I know. I don't really know what to think. I don't have any idea why we're here. I've been trying to figure it out since they shoved us onto the helicopter, but I keep on coming up empty."

Amanda nodded slowly. "Same here. I can't help but wonder if something bigger is underway, something neither of us is seeing. I don't like it."

Kurt picked up a slice of pizza, folded it in half, and took a bite. He was done talking for the moment. They ate in silence for several minutes. Never in Kurt's wildest imagination would he have dreamed of a day like the one he was having. Then again, his life had been a nonstop fiasco since his brother's death. It was just more of the same, he decided. He inhaled his pizza, but only finished half of his cake. Amanda polished off her salad and went back for seconds.

Kurt glanced at his watch as they exited the cafeteria—nine o'clock. He yawned. He didn't know which time zone his body was on at the moment. He supposed Russian. That would explain the fatigue.

"You, too, huh?" Amanda asked, catching his yawn.

"You have no idea."

They passed a conference room crowded with people, their eyes glued to a television with rapt attention. Kurt overheard the CNN theme music.

The sound of high heels approached from their rear. Kurt took Amanda's elbow and guided her to the side of the hall as a young woman in a navy business suit dashed by. She disappeared around the next corner, the click-clack of her heels receding into the distance.

The hallway in front of their quarters was empty. In fact, other than the hurried woman, they hadn't seen anyone.

"Well," Kurt said. "I think I'm going to crash, or try to. I'm wasted." He yawned again.

Amanda leaned against the wall beside her door, raising one leg so her foot was flat against the wall, and her knee was bent. She crossed her arms and gave Kurt a lopsided grin. Her eyes bored into his, locking him in her gaze.

Kurt's heart beat faster, and his palms grew slick. Screwing up his courage, he took a step forward, halving the distance between them.

Amanda straightened, dropping her foot from the wall. She ran her fingers through her hair, brushing it away from her eyes.

"I... uh..." Kurt stammered, suddenly at a loss for words. His confidence faltered.

"It's okay," Amanda breathed. "Really." Her bluntness caught him off guard, and for a second, he hesitated.

Then Amanda pushed herself from the wall and closed the remaining distance. She placed her hands on the sides of his face, leaned in, and planted her lips on his. Kurt marveled at the sensation—soft, yet firm; cool, yet igniting a fire that spread through his entire being. He had been fantasizing about it since he first set eyes on Amanda in London in what seemed a different lifetime.

She melted into his embrace, pressing herself against his body with an intensity that bordered on desperation. Her scent enveloped him, lighting up his senses like fireworks. Kurt tried to maintain control, but he fought a losing battle.

"I wasn't sure..." Amanda murmured into his ear.

Kurt ran his hand along her spine. "I know. Me either..."

Amanda broke the embrace, pushing him back gently. She unclipped her badge and took a step toward the card reader affixed to the wall beside her door. "Do you want to come in?"

Kurt wanted to follow, wanted it with every fiber of his being, but a conflict raged within, a tug of war between what he craved and what he knew—or what he thought he knew—was right. They were colleagues. Entering Amanda's room would change that forever, put them on a course from which there was no return. At the same time, how could he ignore the attraction? It was a visceral thing, born of shared sacrifice and survival against all odds. *If this is wrong, then what is right?* he thought.

As he was about to succumb, a Klaxon horn blared two sharp blasts followed by a longer third. After a brief pause, the sequence repeated.

"What the...?" Kurt looked around, searching for source of the noise.

A young man's voice crackled over the public address system speaker mounted in the ceiling. "Attention. Kurt Vetter and Amanda Carter. Please report to the Presidential operations center immediately."

The moment was gone. Whatever was going on

between them would have to wait. For now. Kurt saw the disappointment in Amanda's eyes, and he shared her pain.

"Which way?" he asked, taking a step back from her door.

"Follow the red line." Amanda pointed at a thick fire-engine red line painted on the floor.

They took off at a sprint.

EIGHT

Mount Weather, Virginia
Presidential Operations Center

AMANDA DID A QUICK HEAD count. The room was packed with people, the air thick with the electric buzz of the unfolding crisis. President Cooper huddled in one corner with Dominic Velasquez and a small contingent of senior military people. Several well-dressed civilians, none of whom she recognized, sat around a small conference table with a phone on it, arguing over something. Uniformed service personnel manned computer workstations lining two of the walls.

A high-definition video screen covered the far wall, stretching from the floor to the edge of the ceiling. Amanda blinked. It appeared as if the operations center extended into another, larger space, a room complete with bright windows and a view of a lawn beyond. *Video conference*, she realized.

Two people sat at a conference table on the remote end of the video link. One, an older grandfatherlylooking gentleman with tufts of white hair ringing his head and thick metal-rimmed glasses, looked into the camera. The other was a young woman, petite, with the posture of a lifelong athlete. She wore stylish horn-rimmed glasses and had her shoulder-length blond hair tied back in a ponytail. She tapped at a computer, murmuring to herself the entire time.

"Wow," Kurt said from behind Amanda. His fingers brushed the small of her back, sending a wave of pleasant shivers up her spine.

Despite the gravity of the situation, Amanda couldn't shake the thoughts of what had almost happened. They had been so close. She had been waiting for Kurt to make a move, wondering if he ever would. He was obviously interested. Everything about the way he looked at her screamed it. She was relieved they had finally broken the ice, even if she had to be the one to do the breaking. If it weren't for the damned alarm, the night may have gone somewhere interesting. She sighed inwardly. *There's always later.*

It had taken her years to achieve a sense of peace with herself and what she did for a living, and the phone call from Kurt a week earlier had undone all of it in a matter of seconds. Mike Vetter, her longtime friend and colleague, and Kurt's brother, was dead, murdered by his own government. But that wasn't the worst of it. It turned out that Mike had been involved with a rogue element of the CIA intent upon reviving the Cold War.

If Kurt's information had come from anyone other than Mike, she would have dismissed it out of hand, but she trusted Mike with her life. They shared a long history, a bond not unlike the one she had developed with Kurt in Moscow, but without the romantic angle. Unlike Kurt, Mike had been happily married, dedicated to his wife and children and was intent upon staying that way, despite Amanda's offer early in their relationship.

Dominic glanced in their direction and cracked an easy smile. He whispered something to President Cooper, then waved Kurt and her over.

"Here we go," Kurt said.

Amanda followed him over to the dignitaries.

The President extended his hand. "Thanks for coming." They engaged in a perfunctory round of handshakes. "We've got some new information about the attack on our networks, and I want to bring you up to speed and get your take on it."

Kurt cleared his throat and shot Amanda a questioning glance. "Before we get started, sir, and I don't mean any disrespect, but I'm... *we're* a little confused. Neither Ms. Carter nor myself are experts at this sort of thing. I appreciate your confidence in our abilities, but I'm not sure what we can bring to the table."

President Cooper stared at Kurt for a heartbeat, then let out a short laugh. "You don't get it, do you?"

Amanda bit her lip. "I'm not sure I follow you, sir."

The President gestured at the room, at the people working at the computers, the soldiers barking orders. "I had a long talk with Director Pungley at the CIA. Things are a mess over there right now. We're pretty sure we've identified all of our people involved in the Moscow incident, but until the dust settles, I don't trust any of them. Neither does the director. There are ongoing operations that must be maintained—Afghanistan, for example—but for something like this, I want people I know and trust running things."

Amanda couldn't believe what she was hearing. The President was placing his trust in her and Kurt, bypassing all of the normal chains of command. He was going to piss off a *lot* of people.

"There are other people involved, of course," the President added. He gestured at the screen. "That's Charlie Howell and Darlene Foster at the National Security Agency. You spoke to them earlier on the helicopter."

Amanda looked at the screen. Charlie and Darlene were both watching the camera, waiting for the video conference to start.

"But what about—" Kurt began.

President Cooper cut him off. "Whatever you're worrying about—stop. You're part of this operation. I'll brief the necessary people. If there are any problems, they'll have to come through me first." He focused his attention on Amanda. "And Ms. Carter, I know there are some issues we have to resolve with your people in Ottawa, but once those are behind us, I want to assure you that you have a place on this team."

Amanda swallowed hard. Up until that moment, she had been avoiding thoughts of Ottawa and the inevitable confrontation that awaited her. Despite Kurt's prodding, she had resisted revealing her nationality, partly out of habit and partly because she didn't want to answer the questions that were sure to follow. Her very presence inside Mount Weather spoke volumes about the precarious relationship she shared with the United States.

The daughter of an American diplomat and a Canadian concert pianist, she had spent most of her early years attending private schools in the United States. During her final year at Harvard, she was approached simultaneously by the CIA and the Canadian Security Intelligence Service, or CSIS. Both agencies were interested in her linguistic and technical skills, and a brief, yet intense courtship ensued. Amanda struggled mightily with the decision of which service best suited her goals, and after a long and painful bout of soul-searching, she came to the conclusion the Canadians were the best fit. While smaller and less well-equipped than their American counterpart, they were far more nimble, and Amanda felt she would have more opportunity to grow and have an impact there. The CIA wasn't done with her, however, and she found out later that they had brokered a deal with the CSIS, allowing them access to her skills under certain unspecified conditions.

"Thank you, sir," she said, meaning it.

Kurt turned to her, a look of bemusement on his face. "You're Canadian? Why didn't you say so?"

Amanda shrugged. "I wanted to, but... it's complicated."

As she had expected, Kurt wasn't satisfied. "I don't understand—"

"I'll tell you all about it later," she said, trying to steer the conversation back to President Cooper, who was observing their interchange with a curious grin.

~ * * * ~

The President kicked off the conference call with the NSA a few minutes later, starting with a quick round of introductions. Then, he launched straight into the subject of the meeting.

"So what do you guys have for us?"

On the screen, Charlie and Darlene looked at each other. Charlie gestured at Darlene, giving her the floor.

"We've made good progress in the past hour," Darlene said, glancing at her computer. "Like I said earlier, the attack originated from within a cluster of servers in a Pentagon data center, and spread from there. We've traced through the entire network, as well as all other systems on the periphery, those that exhibited no signs of activity during the attack, and it appears the damage is isolated to the SEWS network."

Kurt noticed President Cooper didn't relax at the news.

"I assume you have access logs," Dominic interjected.

A satisfied smile grew on Darlene face. "We do."

"In that case," Dominic continued. "Who was it?"

Darlene tilted her head at her boss. "Charlie?"

Charlie cleared his throat. "Once we narrowed it down to a specific group of servers in the Pentagon data center, it wasn't difficult to isolate the source system. The code was introduced to a file server two days ago, when it was brought down for routine maintenance. A tech named Melody Jackson installed a set of security patches, then brought the system back on line. We believe she introduced the worm during this window."

President Cooper pinched the bridge of his nose. "And where is Ms. Jackson now?"

Charlie blinked. "Unknown. No one has seen her since yesterday morning. She called in sick. We sent an FBI team to her condo in Bethesda, and there was no sign of her. No signs of struggle, either..."

"What about cell phone traffic?" Kurt offered. "Computer traffic? Believe me, I know how hard it is to disappear these days." He thought of his most recent trip to South America, where despite the distance in miles and culture, he still hadn't been able to escape the news of his brother's death.

"Nothing," Darlene admitted with an annoyed frown.

President Cooper turned to Dominic. "Is there anyone else we should bring in?"

Dominic chewed his lip. "No. Not really. We've got the right people involved now. The NSA is the best at this sort of thing. They're working around the clock."

President Cooper shifted his attention to Kurt. "What do you think, Mr. Vetter?"

Kurt's mind raced. It was his opportunity to shine. President Cooper was asking for *his* advice. "Well... since she's gone dark, I believe we should assume the worst."

"And that is?"

"She's dead. Whoever orchestrated the attack killed her so she couldn't talk." Kurt held his breath, waiting for someone, anyone, to object to his analysis. The call went silent while everyone digested his idea.

"Dominic," President Cooper said finally. "We need to dig into Ms. Jackson's background, find out who she knew and who they knew. Someone out there has information on her whereabouts. We need to find them."

Dominic pulled out a phone. "I'm calling the FBI right now."

"Meanwhile," President Cooper said. "What about the SEWS? Are we blind?"

Dominic paused and looked up from his phone. "Not at all, sir. We're running on a disaster recovery instance. An instance, I may add, without Ms. Jackson's patches."

"Good." President Cooper smiled for the first time.

The conference call dragged on for another two hours with Kurt and Amanda mostly acting as observers. By the time it was over, Kurt wasn't any clearer on his role, and by the bored look on Amanda's face, she wasn't either.

Finally, President Cooper called for a half-hour break, and everyone scattered for the bathrooms and fresh coffee.

The clock was ticking, and they were getting nowhere fast.

NINE

Mount Weather, Virginia
Presidential Operations Center
Thirty One Minutes Later

"WHILE WE WERE ON BREAK, I thought about what I said earlier, about how I want Mr. Vetter and Ms. Carter to be central to this investigation. I believe, and Dominic concurs," President Cooper said, looking at Dominic and receiving a tilted head in agreement, "that we need to be more formal than I had originally intended, to make sure there's no confusion as to who is in charge."

"I want you to run this show," he continued, fixing his gaze on Kurt. "You've got the background, the agency contacts, and the credibility, notwithstanding the events after your wife's death, to make things happen."

Kurt winced at the mention of Amelia. She and his daughter Heidi had both died in an automobile crash six months earlier.

President Cooper shifted his focus to Amanda. "Ms.

Carter. You'll report to Mr. Vetter in a special advisory capacity."

Amanda opened her mouth to say something, and then closed it.

"Did you have something to add?" the President asked.

"No, sir. I'm sure we can work it all out."

"Good. Ms. Foster," he said, addressing the video screen. Darlene was alone; Charlie hadn't returned after the break. "Your situation is a bit more difficult. You will also report directly to Mr. Vetter. From this moment on, consider yourself on indefinite loan from the National Security Agency. They're going to struggle without you over there, but this is more important."

Darlene nodded. "Yes, sir."

President Cooper turned back to Kurt. "Now, Mr. Vetter, you're officially working for me, but you'll report to Dom. He and I go back a long way, and I trust him with my life. You should, too."

"Understood." It seemed like the right thing to say, even though Kurt didn't really understand.

"All of the resources of this country are at your disposal. Intelligence, military, and civilian. Anything you need. If you need eyes over Assholeistan in twenty minutes, it's yours. If you want a load of paratroopers dropped into the center of Bangkok, it's yours. Just ask."

Kurt was blown away by the power being offered. It was unprecedented. Or maybe it wasn't. Since he had never been in such a situation, he had no idea.

"I'll run interference with Congress and the oversight people. You have free rein to do whatever you need in order to catch these sons-of-bitches and put them in the ground. Fast."

It was a side of President Cooper that Kurt had never seen before, never even imagined.

"Sir?" he asked, trying to project an air of confidence he didn't feel. "This probably doesn't bear asking, but what do you mean by *fast*?"

President Cooper chuckled and shared a knowing glance with Dominic. "I told you he was quick." His face turned deadly serious. "By fast, I mean *yesterday*. No one attacks us and gets away with it. No one."

"Understood." Kurt made brief eye contact with Amanda, a flood of understanding passing between them as their budding relationship was smothered under their new roles.

Darlene raised her hand. "What about access to NSA resources?"

"Done," President Cooper barked. "Everything you had yesterday, you have today, except none of the red-tape bureaucratic bullshit."

Darlene smiled. "Thank you, sir."

"Now, I'm sure you have a million questions, Mr. Vetter. Dom is prepared to answer them and help you get up and running."

Kurt looked at Dominic, who gave him an enthusiastic thumbs-up.

President Cooper rapped his knuckles on the table. "If you'll excuse me, I have a few phone calls to make before we head back to D.C." He got up and exited the room, leaving Kurt, Amanda, Darlene, and Dominic to fend for themselves.

"Back to D.C.?" Amanda asked.

"We got the all-clear from the Secret Service," Dominic announced. "We're heading back in about an hour."

Kurt took a deep breath and tried to put on his most confident face. "I guess we'd better get started then."

"My thoughts exactly." Dominic got to his feet and crossed the room to a white board stretching the entire length of the wall. He grabbed a handful of markers and threw one to each of the others at the table. "We've got a long night ahead of us. Spinning up an operation like this requires a ton of people and ridiculous amounts of coordination. The first thing we need to do is hash out a preliminary organizational structure so everyone knows who is in charge."

With a few quick strokes, he drew a series of boxes representing President Cooper's vision, with the President at the top of the stack and Kurt, Amanda, and Darlene at the bottom, separated only by himself. He took a step back to check his work. "This is our structure," he said, turning to the group. "Work with it, and we'll get this done."

"We'll need some support staff," Kurt volunteered. "Security, administrative, that kind of thing." He went to the board and added his ideas. He paused for a moment, and then shook his head. "I'm sure I'm missing something."

"Don't worry. It's a good start," Dominic said.

"What about facilities?" Amanda asked. "We'll need a base of operations with access to people and a host of classified networks, both domestic and foreign."

Dominic looked thoughtful. "I'm open."

"How about somewhere in Maryland?" she suggested. "Close to DC and the NSA, with easy access to transportation."

"We need the ability to travel quickly, on short notice," Kurt chimed in.

"Not a problem," Dominic said. "You'll have an airplane on standby at Andrews Air Force Base, with a team of military pilots ready to take you wherever you need to go."

Kurt marveled at the potential.

Dominic added, "Really, anything you need."

Kurt realized Darlene hadn't voiced her opinion yet.

"What do you think, Darlene?"

"Maryland is good. It would be convenient to have quick access to the resources at the Fort," she said, referring to Fort Meade, the home of the National Security Agency.

Dominic chewed his lip. "That's too bad. I already had the perfect place for you in Fairfax. You'd be surrounded by government infrastructure, and Dulles airport is right next door. There's even an office building available, already wired for all of the necessary networks." He thought for a moment. "How about Annapolis? I think we can find space for you at The Naval Academy. Like Fairfax, it's fully wired, and I believe we have facilities available. BWI is right up the road. It's a little more remote than Fairfax, but that could play in our favor since it's not as well known, and less likely to become a target."

"I like Annapolis," Amanda said. "But I can work anywhere, and I expect I'll be in the field most of the time anyway."

Kurt hadn't considered that. "Annapolis it is," he said, making his first executive decision.

Dominic smiled. "Good. I think you'll like it there. The facility is on the eastern edge of the city, right off Route 50." He returned to his seat.

"How do we get things rolling?" Kurt asked.

Dominic held up a finger. "That's where I come in. You tell me what you need, and I'll make sure it appears as fast as possible. I want you to focus on catching the hacker." He picked up a secure phone line and dialed. "This is Dominic. Set up a meeting with Commander Simpson at the Naval Academy as soon as possible. Uh huh. Uh huh. Thanks." He hung up.

"Done."

"That was almost too easy," Kurt said.

"Oh, nothing about this will be easy. It just looks that way from where you're sitting."

With their initial logistics settled, the new team broke up to prepare for their return to civilization.

TEN

National Security Agency, Sector C
0600, The Next Morning

DARLENE POPPED HER HEAD INTO Charlie's office. Empty.

She continued to her office, just down the hall, and spent a few minutes collecting her belongings and sending emails to coworkers, informing them of her departure. She was slightly annoyed that no one was around to say goodbye, but not surprised. People worked strange hours in the NSA, herself included. She would catch up later.

According to Dom—she still couldn't believe she was on a first name basis with the National Security Advisor—she would have the same connections available at the Annapolis facility, so she really wouldn't be that far away. That was the only positive. Otherwise, she was conflicted on the idea of moving south. Granted, it would cut her commute by ten minutes, but it also meant adding a lot of other hassle to her life, bureaucratic headaches she had previously avoided.

She heard footsteps in the hallway behind her. Checking the mirror taped to the top right corner of her primary monitor, she saw Charlie Howell approaching. He wore a sad smile, yet the twinkle in his eyes and the way he carried himself, head held high and shoulders back, said something entirely different. Darlene swiveled around and stood, thrilled to have the opportunity to see him in person before she departed.

"I'm so glad I caught you!" Charlie said, opening his arms. He wore a button-down shirt with the top three buttons undone, faded jeans, and scuffed blue leather hiking boots. The vestiges of his hair were a mess, flying every direction as if he had been tugging at it all night.

Darlene forced a smile, trying to disguise the sadness she felt at leaving. Charlie had been a great boss, maybe even her best. She would miss working with him, especially the latitude he gave her to do her job the way she saw fit. It had been a calculated gamble on his part, and one that had paid off in spades. Darlene knew she was the star performer in his organization, the golden goose that he trotted out during quarterly performance reviews with his superiors. Not that Charlie had to worry too much about his budget. His group, like the one she was leaving to join, had been created by special presidential directive, and enjoyed a tremendous degree of support from the President himself.

Charlie enveloped her in a great bear hug, squeezing her so tight her back cracked. He was a touchy-feely manager, a personality trait she had despised at first, but had grown to accept and even appreciate during her tenure. From Kurt's body language, she guessed he didn't operate the same way.

He was more standoffish.

"So, they're stealing you away?" Charlie asked as he released her.

She nodded. "Unfortunately, yes. The President said it's only temporary, though."

Charlie laughed. "Right. Next thing you know, you'll have your own group, and I'll be working for you."

Darlene blushed. "I don't think you have to worry about that."

"I hear you're setting up shop in Annapolis."

Word travels fast, Darlene thought, amused. "They're putting us up in an unused naval facility."

He nodded enthusiastically. "Good. I'm happy for you, Darlene. You deserve this."

Darlene wasn't sure how to respond. She knew she was good at her job. She had demonstrated that repeatedly—most recently with her analysis of the Moscow bomb—but whether she deserved it or not was a different question altogether.

"We'll see." She glanced around her workspace. "I think I've got everything." She hefted her bag onto her shoulder. Inside was a pair of battered paperbacks, horror novels she kept in her desk for the late nights when she was waiting for data runs to complete. Working in a secure environment, she wasn't allowed to bring anything electronic, so she had no CD player, iPod, or digital picture frames—none of the normal accouterments of the typical American cubicle worker.

"Is there anything else I can do for you on this end?" Charlie asked.

Darlene looked around. "Keep my seat warm. I'll be back."

Charlie rolled his eyes, and then his expression became serious. "If you don't seize this opportunity and run with it, I'll consider it a personal failure."

Darlene was confused. “What do you mean?”

“You really don’t get it, do you? The President has asked for you personally to run a massive data collection effort, to be his point person in what is probably the most important job in the country right now. If you do well at this, and I’m sure you will, you can write your own ticket. Your career is set for life.”

Darlene gulped. She hadn’t considered it that way. He had a point. Part of it was her age. At twenty-nine, she hadn’t thought that far ahead. She enjoyed her work, sifting through data, looking for patterns. The career aspect had happened without any conscious effort. Deep down, she knew that wasn’t the typical progression of a young analyst inside her organization. Most toiled in obscurity for years, lost in complex mathematical formulas and computer programs, without ever seeing the light of day.

“I’ll keep that in mind,” she assured him. “Meanwhile, do you want to walk out with me?”

He shook his head. “I’d love to, but I’ve got a meeting with the department heads. Drop me a line when you get settled.”

Darlene smiled. “I will.”

After another quick hug, she left her former office and set out on the path to her new life.

ELEVEN

Washington, DC
At The Same Time

VIKTOR TILTED THE BLOOD-SPLATTERED Lexan safety shield back from his face and placed his cordless reciprocating saw on the edge of the ten-by-twelve blue tarp covering the work area. His arms ached, partly from the weight of the tool and partly because he had been sawing nonstop for the past twenty minutes.

In hindsight, he wished he had purchased a larger tarp. *Next time*, he told himself. He lifted a corner of the tarp and held it aloft for a second. The small river of blood heading toward him reversed course and raced back toward the center, where it pooled around Melody Jackson's remains.

Though not the first time he had killed, it was the first time he had dismembered a victim. He had seen it done before in the movies, and he had even practiced on a steer at a farm on the eastern shore of Maryland so he would have a good feel for what to expect. Still, the actual act performed on a person was far more revolting, and at the same time, far easier than he had expected. He closed his eyes and pictured Melody at their last meeting, the day before she had injected the worm into the DoD computer systems.

They had met at a coffee shop in Adams Morgan, neutral ground for both of them. Melody, dressed for work in her Marine uniform that offset her lustrous auburn hair, had seemed resigned about the task ahead. She must have known, Viktor thought, the repercussions of her actions. Those systems were too well audited for anyone to do what she did and get away with it. Unless she added a little something extra to the mix, something that would erase her tracks and allow her to escape undetected...

He still marveled at how easy it had been to bring her under his influence. A few lines of coke late one night after his bar closed, a discreet digital camera, and she had been his. She had objected at first, threatened to report him to her supervisors and to reveal the extent of her debauchery, but in the end, Viktor had convinced her that the impact of her work for him would pale in comparison to the impact on her life and career if the truth got out. She *wanted* to believe her lapse in judgment would go away by performing another. It was an age-old trick in Viktor's repertoire, one he had used countless times.

Killing Melody had been easy. The day after she finished with the computer systems, she called in sick to work and sent him a text informing him of her status. He instructed her to gather all of her things and meet him at a Super 8 on the Maryland side of the border. There, he had told her, he would provide her with the original recordings and release her from her obligation. One thing was certain; if it hadn't been Melody, he would have found someone else. Maybe not right away, but eventually. Everyone had a weakness, and it was just a matter of figuring out what it was and how to exploit it.

Reaching around, Viktor picked up one of the seven heavy-duty industrial trash bags he had prepared earlier. He slid his fingers into the top edge of the bag and snapped it open, taking care not to dip it into Melody's blood.

First in was the head. "Sorry," he said as he dug his fingers into her hair and turned it so he couldn't see her eyes. The head landed in the bag with a sick *plop.*

Viktor pulled the drawstring on the bag, securing it, and then placed it to the side. He deposited the arms and legs into separate bags, saving her torso for last. The torso was much harder to maneuver due to its weight and the lack of appendages to hold. Viktor's hands were slick with blood by the time he finally got it tucked into its own bag and out of sight. He pulled a handful of red shop rags from an open box and wiped as much blood from his hands and clothes as he could, then did the same with the trash bags containing Melody's body parts.

The last remaining evidence of his crime was the plastic sheeting. Taking care not to spill more blood, he folded it over onto itself until it was a small one-by-one-foot square. He deposited it in the final trash bag, leaving the top open.

Viktor inspected himself. Blood slicked the heavy gray butcher's apron tied at his waist. His pants legs, below the cover of the apron, were soaked through, almost black, glistening in the harsh fluorescent light. The rubber military surplus rain boots on his feet were a mottled red and green, the color of week-old meat left in the sun.

He stripped, placing each item of clothing into the

trash bag. He detached the blade from the saw and dropped it, along with the face shield, on top of his clothes. With a satisfied tug, he drew the bag shut and tied the strings.

Viktor surveyed the room, searching for any missed evidence. Not seeing anything, he picked up a fat green garden hose and turned the spray on himself, washing away the stray smears of blood, sending pink rivers of water down the rusty drain in the center of the floor. He would take a long, hot shower when he got home, he decided, probably the longest of his life. He toweled off with a thin camp towel, then dressed in a pair of jeans and a t-shirt bearing the Washington Capitals logo. He slipped his feet into a pair of leather sandals.

Pleased with the results of his work, Viktor loaded the trash bags into the back of his Ford Expedition. He had a few hours of driving ahead as he made the rounds to several local trash incinerators, facilities he had scoped out weeks before and arranged for access to with small amounts of cash. Within two hours, all traces of Melody Jackson would be gone, up in smoke.

Once that was complete, he would go home, pour himself a stiff drink or three, and try to forget. Tomorrow in Baltimore, he had to do it all over again, with Greg Miller. But he knew it would get easier. In the world of murder, Viktor had joined an elite club, and oddly enough, he felt proud.

Twirling his keys around his finger, he made his way to the driver's side of the Expedition. He roared off into the night with an eager grin.

TWELVE

Annapolis, Maryland
Noon

DARLENE PULLED INTO THE EMPTY lot of the Annapolis facility, parking her two-year-old black Volkswagen beetle between a white Verizon panel truck and a shiny government SUV. Kurt and Amanda were still in D.C., taking care of personnel issues; she had been sent ahead to their new facilities to oversee the initial setup.

Getting out of the car, she cast her eyes at her destination, a foreboding three-story gray stone building with narrow, dark glass windows recessed like archer ports in a medieval castle. The windows, she knew, were only for show. Behind them, a mesh of wire and a host of other materials wove together to prevent radio signals from leaking.

According to Dominic, the building had originally been used for signal analysis. Run by naval intelligence, it had been out of commission for a little over five years, just long enough for the internal systems to be on the edge of obsolescence. That explained the presence of the Verizon truck. The contractors, vetted by the government and cleared to work in secure environments, were in the midst of establishing connectivity to the various networks she would need to do her job.

A pair of armed Marines stood guard at the door, protecting the only entrance into and out of the building. Taking her badge, they ran it under a laser scanner, then asked her to place her eyes against a retina scanner. Darlene complied without a second thought, waiting for the green light to flash and the machine to beep. She was used to the procedure from her job at NSA.

Once inside the building, she made her way to the rear of the first floor, where their offices were located. Kurt's office was first, and peeking in, she saw a bored Marine watching one of the Verizon contractors connect cables to a desktop computer.

She continued past the next set of offices—Amanda's and hers—to the conference room, dominated by a chipped and battered 1970s-era laminated oak table and a full complement of rolling chairs, some broken, some whole.

Boxes littered the conference table. Digital projectors, new telephone systems, and several computers, were stacked according to function. A pile of flattened cardboard lay in one corner, remains of equipment already unpacked.

"Can I help you?"

She turned, startled. A naval officer stood behind her, a clipboard in one hand and an annoyed expression on his face.

"I'm Darlene Foster." She held out her hand.

The man relaxed and shook her hand. "I'm sorry. I was told you'd be here later this afternoon. We're still putting things together. I'm Lieutenant Milgram."

She suppressed a grin. "It's nice to meet you." She looked around. "You work fast."

Lieutenant Milgram chuckled. "We try. Let me give you the guided tour. I've got a few minutes before I have to head off to a meeting."

Darlene was more than a little impressed with how fast the preparations had been undertaken. It spoke volumes as to the importance of what they were doing. Her excitement was genuine, yet tempered by a twinge of nervousness. Could she live up to the President's expectations? Did she even want to? Truth be told, she had little choice. He was depending on her, along with Kurt and Darlene, to hunt down the hackers and stop them before they could strike again. The time to decline the offer, if there had ever been one, had long since passed.

"That sounds great!" She fell into step behind him, trailing him down the long hall.

They spent the next ten minutes moving from room to room, figuring out where to put people, and what else they needed to get up and running. According to Kurt, support personnel would be on site within twenty-four hours, which would give them the infrastructure to start organizing.

They ended beside the front door.

Lieutenant Milgram glanced at his watch. "Well, that's all for now. Feel free to do whatever you need. Just watch out for the workmen."

Darlene smiled. "I will. Thanks again."

The sergeant's face grew serious. "Good luck with whatever you're doing here. I've never seen this much of a rush on a job before."

Darlene shrugged in response. "Thanks."

The sergeant slipped through the door and was gone. Alone, Darlene spun on her heel and headed to her office. She wanted to get online and start working. Sergeant Milgram had told her that the contractors had been briefed to complete construction on her office first.

She took a seat behind her new desk, spinning around in the chair once to test it out, then leaning back and fiddling with the controls until she found the knob for the height. She dropped the chair a few inches and grinned, satisfied. *Not as nice as my desk at Fort Meade, but it'll do.*

She wiggled her mouse, and the trio of monitors arrayed on her desk flickered to life, displaying the over-sized logo of the secure intelligence network where she would spend most of her time in the coming days and weeks.

It was time to get to work.

THIRTEEN

Hyatt Regency
Washington, DC

AMANDA SPIT TOOTHPASTE INTO THE sink and rinsed her mouth with a handful of cold water. Taking a towel from the rack beside the sink, she patted her face dry. She took a step back, inspecting herself in the full-length mirror on the back of the bathroom door. Dressed in lightweight brown pants, a short-sleeved cream blouse, and a pair of strappy leather heels, she thought she looked acceptable for a full day of meetings with government officials. Reaching into her purse, she dug around until she found a hair clip. She pulled her shoulder-length hair back into a ponytail, fastening it close to her head. That would keep her hair off her neck, a necessity in the late-August D.C. weather. She checked the mirror a final time. *Good enough.* She grabbed her bags and left her room, making sure to flip the placard on the doorknob from *Do not disturb* to *Clean.*

Her room was midway down the hall on the fourth

floor, only a few doors away from the expansive bank of elevators. Her heels made a staccato *click-clack* on the polished marble floors as she crossed over from the carpet. It was a little after eight, and she wasn't scheduled to meet Kurt until eight thirty. Their first appointment of the morning was at nine thirty, in Dominic's office at the White House. She wanted to grab a cup of tea before she saw Kurt, and collect her thoughts about what was going on between them.

The moment in the hallway at Mount Weather replayed on a continuous loop, one moment filling her with hope, and the next with crushing dread. Kurt was the first man in recent memory who had stirred so much conflict within her, and while it terrified her, it also filled her with a giddy excitement. Working for him would complicate things. The last thing she wanted to do was to cast doubt on the mission, to give the President or Dominic any reason to lose confidence in her, or Kurt's, abilities to do the job.

She looked up at the ceiling. Kurt was somewhere above, on the sixth floor. She wondered if he was still asleep. *Probably.* He didn't seem like the kind of man who spent much time worrying about what to wear for a meeting.

The elevator arrived with a soft chime, and the door rumbled open. Amanda stepped inside and pressed the button for the first floor. A few moments later the doors opened, revealing the well-appointed lobby. They had a full agenda for the day, with meetings all morning in downtown D.C., then heading to Annapolis to see their new offices for the first time. The goal for the morning was to finalize the staff they would need for their investigation, both military and civilian, and to kick off the process of reassignment.

Amanda spied her goal, a small coffee stand, on the far side of the lobby, near the front door. She set off in that direction.

A few minutes later, she sat on a plush couch near the front door, a steaming paper cup of Earl Grey in one hand and her mobile phone in the other. She spent a minute checking the news headlines, flicking through screens with her thumb, moving from topic to topic in rapid-fire fashion. She smiled as she read the explanation of the White House evacuation on Google News. The media attributed the event to a routine continuity of operations exercise, an obscure new government policy instituted in the wake of the 9/11 attacks. She clicked on a link to a transcript of an interview with the White House press secretary, where he apologized to the residents of the district for causing undue alarm with their 'routine emergency planning exercise.'

She blew on her tea to cool it, then took a short sip. She set the cup on the end table to her right and returned her attention to her phone.

"Excuse me, Ms. Carter?"

Amanda looked up and saw a well-dressed man in a blue suit sitting across from her. She hadn't noticed him arrive. "Do I know you?" she asked. Something about his accent set off alarm bells, something she couldn't quite identify.

The man reached into the breast pocket of his suit jacket and withdrew a billfold. He flipped it open, and Amanda saw the familiar logo of the Canadian Security Intelligence Service. Turning off her phone, she dropped it into her purse and closed the clasp as discreetly as she could.

The man snapped his billfold closed and returned it to his pocket, making an extra effort to make sure Amanda saw the pistol strapped under his armpit. "I don't believe so," he said. "But I know you." He nodded toward someone over her left shoulder. "My associates and I would like a few words with you, if you don't mind."

Amanda glanced over her shoulder and saw two more men standing a few feet away; they were dressed identically to the man seated across from her. She noticed that each man wore a wire snaking from his ear down into the collar of his shirt. That meant there were more operatives somewhere out of sight.

She stole a glance at her watch. Eight twenty. Kurt wasn't due for another ten minutes.

"Anything you have to say, we can discuss right here," she said, injecting far more authority into her voice than she felt.

The man smiled. "I wish that were the case. We have a car out front. You're going to come with me. If you try anything... well, just don't. I have orders to bring you in dead or alive."

Amanda's mind raced as she considered her options. She could bolt, head for the stairs and try to outrun the men. However, they most likely had all of the exits covered. That was what she would do in their position. The other option was to yell, cause a scene and act as if she were being attacked, which unfortunately she was, only in a more civilized manner. She studied the agent's face, his eyes, and the tight line of his lips. He wasn't bluffing. Creating a scene would cause problems she couldn't foresee.

"Now," the man ordered, his voice dropping an octave.

Amanda cast her gaze toward the elevators. *Still no Kurt.*

A new plan began to materialize. She would go with the CSIS men, then run once she got outside. She would be in the open, with all of the traffic and commotion of early-morning D.C. to disguise her direction once she got free.

"Okay. Do you mind if I bring my tea?"

The man chuckled. "I don't think so."

Too bad. It would have made a good weapon. Amanda got to her feet and retrieved her purse. She took one last look at the elevators before turning toward the front doors. The first man fell in behind her while the other two moved into flanking positions, maintaining a casual distance, but staying close enough to respond to any sudden movements.

As she pushed through the main door, her hopes evaporated. A gray Ford delivery van, skinny and tall like something from the streets of Europe, idled at the curb with its cavernous side door wide open. A man and a woman, also impeccably dressed, stood on either side of the door, their gazes alternating between the approaching party and the pedestrian traffic on New Jersey Avenue.

Amanda seethed. To get so close and to have it all snatched away made her furious. Yet she was powerless to fight the events which had taken hold of her, unable to do anything but be swept along until a better opportunity to act presented itself.

The CSIS agents guided her into the van, one of them slamming the door closed with a rumbling *bang*. Before she was even seated, the driver, a young man with short sandy hair and a light beard, gunned the gas. He injected them into the flow of cars, turning them into yet another anonymous vehicle in the maelstrom of D.C. traffic.

~ * * * ~

Kurt exited the stairwell into the lobby and checked his watch. Eight thirty-four. He scanned the cavernous room, searching for Amanda, and raised a curious eyebrow when he didn't spot her right away. She was usually on time or early.

Spying a group of couches near the doors, he took off in that direction. They would give him a good view of the elevators as well as the restroom, in case she had stepped away.

He had been up for three hours, since well before the din of early-morning traffic had climbed the six stories to the thick plate glass window of his room. Despite his exhaustion, he had been unable to let go of the day, unable to reach a point where his mind would disengage and allow him to stop thinking of Amanda and their predicament. He had wanted, with every fiber of his being, to go to her room, to pick up where they had been interrupted at Mount Weather, to spend the night next to her. In the end, he had finally succumbed to a restless approximation of sleep, deferring the decision of whether and how to mix his personal life with his new professional existence until the morning. At some point during the wee hours, he had dreamed of Amanda coming to his room, climbing into his bed, and offering herself to him. However, when he awoke, he was still alone.

As he reached the cluster of couches, he noticed a steaming paper cup on one of the end tables. He looked around and didn't see anyone. Just in case, he took the seat at the other end of the couch.

With another check of his watch, he settled in to wait.

FOURTEEN

Dundalk, Maryland
Around Noon

VIKTOR PULLED INTO THE PARKING lot of the Dundalk Best Western and killed the engine of his Ford Expedition. He sat still for a moment, enjoying the brief silence. Translucent waves of heat shimmered above the buckling parking lot asphalt as far as he could see, reminding him once again how much he hated summer. And how much he loved his air conditioner.

He pulled out his mobile phone and checked for text messages. Greg Miller still hadn't responded to his request for contact, sent a few hours earlier, and Viktor was starting to get worried. He had a bad feeling his job was about to get a whole lot more difficult. Opening the glove compartment, he retrieved his H&K USP 9mm. He pulled the slide to ensure a round was chambered. He could tell from the weight of the pistol that the magazine was full, minus the single bullet he had used on Melody. Leaning forward, he slid the gun into his waistband at his lower back, then pulled his shirt over it.

Waiting was the part of his job he hated most. If things went according to plan, Greg Miller would be in Room 131, a few parking spots away. Viktor would walk in with a smile on his face, act friendly, and then instruct Greg to join him in the Expedition. From there, they would drive to an abandoned warehouse Viktor had scoped out a few days earlier. Then, as with Melody, he would kill the young gambler with a single shot. Maybe two. That was the best case scenario. If things went badly, if Greg fought back, things could get ugly. Viktor didn't mind leaving a little blood behind, as long as it wasn't his.

He popped open the door and climbed out, using the step ladder that extended automatically. His sense of foreboding got worse. There were no other cars in the parking lot. He hadn't instructed Greg to hide his vehicle. That meant Greg was either not there or he was trying to be clever. Viktor hated it when people tried to be clever. It always ended badly.

He reached Greg's room in a few impatient strides. The heavy curtains in the picture window facing the parking lot were closed. His gun dug into his lower spine, and sweat pooled in his armpits, making everything feel slippery and miserable. Planting a congenial smile on his face, Viktor knocked once and took a step back so Greg could see him through the scratched and chipped peephole in the center of the door. A few seconds passed without a response. He knocked again, more insistently.

A tractor-trailer roared by on the highway behind him, the rumble and whoosh of displaced air making the door to Room 131 rattle softly in its frame. Somewhere, a siren blared.

"Damn it!" Viktor set off down the sidewalk,

heading toward the front office. As he pushed into the lobby, a wave of cold, moldy air tinged with industrial cleaners assaulted his nose. He tried to hold his breath.

"Are you checking in?" the thin Hispanic girl behind the front desk chirped.

Viktor swallowed his anger and forced himself to smile again. "No. I'm not." He made a point of checking his watch. "I'm supposed to meet my cousin, Greg Miller, for lunch. He told me he was staying in Room 131, but when I knocked, I got no answer."

The girl moved to her keyboard and hit a few keys. "I'm sorry, sir. We don't have anyone by that name staying with us today. Room 131 is unoccupied."

Viktor leaned on the counter. "Are you sure? Could you check again? Maybe he registered with his wifc's credit card." He slid a twenty-dollar bill across the counter under his palm, and met the girl's eyes. An invisible understanding passed between them as she palmed the money with a nervous glance at a side room.

There's someone else here, Viktor realized. *Maybe a manager.*

The girl returned to her computer and typed furiously, searching, he assumed, for any other guests named Greg or Miller. He wouldn't put it past Greg to try to disguise his identity.

Viktor waited patiently, allowing his eyes to roam the area behind the counter. He heard the sound of a door closing in another room, and a moment later, a young man about the same age as the girl emerged. He nodded at Viktor. "Good afternoon, sir."

Viktor returned the nod. "Hey."

The man collected a tall stack of credit card receipts from beside the girl and retreated into the back office.

After what seemed an eternity, the girl stopped typing. "I'm sorry, sir. I've searched for all guests with similar names at our location and at the other Best Westerns in the metro area, and there's no record."

She moved to pass the money back to Viktor, but he waved her off. "Keep it."

"Thanks," she said with a nervous smile.

"Well..." Viktor said. "I guess something must have come up." He straightened and pulled his keys from his pocket. "I'll give him a call, then, and find out what happened."

"I hope everything is all right," the girl offered.

Viktor hesitated for a second, unsure what to do next. "Yes. I'm sure he's fine. Thank you for your trouble."

The girl smiled. "No trouble at all, sir. Have a good day."

Once outside, Viktor scanned the parking lot again on the off chance Greg had arrived while he was inside. Nothing. Just as he had feared, Greg had bolted. Where he had gone, Viktor had no idea. From their discussions about the loan, he knew Greg didn't have a lot of resources.

Viktor's thoughts turned dark. He would have to call his superiors, and he would have to do it soon. Yesterday, he had told them everything was under control. With Greg's disappearance, things most definitely were not under control. Not that he was worried. Melody had been his primary concern. She had had access to the White House with a top-level security clearance and military service records stretching back several years. There was a good chance someone could have tied them together. Greg, on the other hand, was a wild card, an unknown. Viktor had no connection to him other than their financial arrangement and the work he had done to pay off his debt. If Greg was like other gamblers Viktor knew, he would be too embarrassed at his situation to disclose it to anyone. That was potentially good for Viktor because it meant there were unlikely to be any ties that could connect him. At the same time, it made things more difficult because there was no one he could lean on to learn of Greg's location.

He returned to the Expedition, got inside, and fired it up. The air conditioner came on with a roar, drowning out his thoughts. He pulled his gun from his waistband and returned it to the glove box. He had to find Greg Miller, and he had to find him fast.

Slipping the transmission into reverse, Viktor pulled out of his parking spot, his mind already fifty miles away, inside Greg Miller's house.

FIFTEEN

Hyatt Regency Washington
Washington, DC

"SHE'S GONE? WHAT DO YOU mean, *she's gone*?"

Kurt switched his phone to his other ear. "According to the people at the front desk, she left a few minutes before I came downstairs. And she wasn't alone."

"Shit!" Dominic said. "Did the hotel staff get a look at the people who took her? Enough for a description?"

Kurt sighed, exasperated. "No. The woman at the front desk said they were well dressed. She's pretty sure one of them ate breakfast in the hotel restaurant earlier. That pretty much describes most of the men walking around D.C."

"Really? Did you—"

Kurt cut him off. "I already asked. He paid in cash."

"Damn it!"

Kurt leaned against the reception counter and glared in the general direction of the lobby where he was supposed to have met Amanda. "Who the hell knew she was here? And why would anyone want to take her?" He knew the answer to the second question before he asked it. Amanda was bound to have more enemies than he could count, given her occupation, some who would even want her dead. The first part of the question, however, remained unanswered. No one could have known she was there, and more specifically, that she would be in the lobby at the time she was.

Dominic cleared his throat. "The Canadians."

"Excuse me?" Kurt turned to face the mirror behind the front desk.

"I said, the Canadians. It makes sense. Our computers are tied together on multiple levels—immigration, customs, financial. I didn't think much of it at the time, but when you and Amanda first returned from Russia, we received a call from the CSIS, in Ottawa. Their CIA. It came in through back channels; they said they wanted to send some people down here to speak to her."

Kurt could barely contain his anger. "Send some people down here? Why didn't you tell me? Or tell her?" He spun away from the counter, stalked toward the front door, and peered through the tinted glass at the street beyond.

"I'm sorry I didn't tell you. I did, however, speak with Amanda. She didn't seem concerned about it. Like the President said, there were some issues to resolve with her government, and we have people working through them."

Kurt exploded. "Well, they're not doing a very goddamned good job, are they?" He wanted to hurl his phone across the room, to smash it against the reflective marble floor, but bit by bit, he choked back his anger, and finally returned the phone to his ear.

"...down. I'm sure she's okay—"

"Look," Kurt interrupted. "If it's the Canadians, can't you get on the phone with someone and clear it up? Aren't they like... our best friends?"

He stepped to the side as a couple entered the lobby.

"I wish it were that easy," Dominic said. "But if they went to the trouble to send people down here to take her, then I think there's something else going on, something Amanda held back."

You think? "That much is obvious. The question is what? I mean, what could she have done? Why didn't they take her in London? She was there for years. She had an apartment, a car, a life..."

"She wouldn't say," Dominic answered.

Kurt dragged his fingers through his hair. "Can you hold on a second? I want to get Darlene on the call."

"Good idea," Dominic said.

Kurt put Dominic on hold and dialed Darlene. She answered on the first ring.

"Hey," he said before she could get in a word. "I've got Dominic on the other line. We've got a situation here, and we need your help."

"Sure."

Kurt connected the calls. "Dominic? Darlene? Are you still there?"

They were.

"Good. Thanks for joining us, Darlene."

"No problem," she said. "So what's going on?"

"Amanda was abducted. From the hotel. I was wondering if you could put a tracer on her phone. See if it's still broadcasting?"

Darlene gasped. "Abducted? You're kidding! Sure. Give me a second..."

Kurt waited while she worked her magic with the computer systems. "I'm in," she announced a few seconds later.

Kurt asked, "Do you see anything?"

"Just a sec... it looks like her last location was somewhere on New Jersey Avenue, near the Hyatt. Isn't that where you stayed last night?"

Dominic cursed, and Kurt swore he heard the sound of a fist impacting a desk.

"Yeah. That's where I am right now."

"It's odd," Darlene said. "It looks like her last broadcast was a little over an hour ago. Nothing since. She must have turned off her phone."

"Or someone turned it off for her," Dominic added.

Kurt made his way to a couch in the center of the lobby and took a seat. "Dominic thinks it was the Canadians. Evidently, Amanda's unfinished business with them was a lot more serious than she let on."

Dominic coughed. "Is there any other way to track her?"

Kurt pressed his phone against his ear, hoping for good news.

"No," Darlene said, her voice heavy with defeat. "Without her phone, she's totally off the grid. She may as well not exist."

Kurt bent forward and stared vacantly at the delicate whorls in the brown and green carpet at his feet, trying in vain to puzzle through Amanda's disappearance. He came up short.

She was gone.

Resignation flooded through him, and his shoulders sagged. "So what now? How do we get her back?"

Darlene said, "Sorry. I have to drop off. There's a network guy here, and he has some questions. Is there anything else I can do right now?"

"No. I don't think so," Kurt said. "Thanks."

"Call me if you can think of anything else. I should be free in about half an hour."

"Will do," Kurt said. The phone beeped as Darlene left the call.

Kurt got to his feet and returned to the lobby counter. He needed to keep moving, to do something with the anger and frustration percolating inside him. He wanted to scream, vent his frustrations on the nearest person, but he couldn't. Everyone he cared about was dead. And now Amanda was gone, too. He was alone. Again.

"Come to my office," Dominic said. "I'm going to meet with President Cooper as soon as we get off the phone. He'll lean on the Canadians, find out who took her and where they're going. Don't worry."

Kurt barely heard him. "You know, I may just get on a plane and go to Ottawa myself. I could knock on some doors, see if I can find someone who knows something."

Dominic's voice went flat. "You can't do that and you know it."

"And why not?" Kurt asked. "What the hell is stopping me?"

"I'm stopping you. I'm ordering you to stay here in D.C. Do what you need to do, which is finish assembling your team and finding out who hacked us so it doesn't happen again. The President is counting on you. You can't run off to Canada. Not now."

Kurt knew Dominic was right, but he didn't care. He couldn't bear the thought of losing Amanda. "But—"

"No buts. This is an order. Let me work this with the President. We'll get her back. Trust me. The Canadians have too much invested in their relationship with us to pull a stunt like this. I'm sure it's a catch-and-release operation. They'll probably turn her loose in a day or two."

Kurt hated it when people told him to trust them. It

invariably meant he was about to get fucked. He took a deep breath, centered himself, and considered his options. Running off to Canada, while attractive on a visceral level, wasn't really practical. To start with, he didn't have any contacts there. To compound the problem, if it was really the CSIS who had taken her, they certainly weren't going to throw open the doors for him.

"Okay," he said reluctantly. "Forty-eight hours. If you can't get her back in forty-eight hours, I'm going to Canada and find her myself.

Dominic made what sounded like a sigh of relief. "Good. Okay."

"So what am I supposed to do in the meantime?" Kurt asked.

"Your job. Focus on your personnel issues, get your staff in place, and find this hacker."

The fight drained out of Kurt, replaced by a grim sense of obligation. "All right. I get it. I'll deal with this, but let me know as soon as you hear anything. Anything at all."

"Don't worry. You'll be the first to know."

"I hope so, for all our sakes."

SIXTEEN

Outside of Cluj, Romania

MAGOMED SWATTED THE MOSQUITO SLURPING from his hand, crushing its delicate body to a bloody smear. He smiled at his minor victory while wiping his hand on his pants leg. He sat at a dilapidated wooden picnic table under a drooping oak tree at the rear of the building, the only location he had found in the facility where he was able to be alone. He had been there for two hours, flipping through a battered *World Atlas* and taking notes in the small leather-bound journal that never left his side. Another mosquito buzzed him, but Magomed was too slow. It got away.

A soldier rounded the near corner of the facility for the second time in thirty minutes. The man, in his late-twenties with close-cropped brown hair, constantly moving eyes, and an almost imperceptible limp, marched past Magomed without saying a word. He cradled a well-maintained AK-47 in his arms and wore a pistol strapped to his left hip. The guard stopped at the midpoint of the building, and slowly scanned the tree line.

Magomed perked up, curious as to what the man had seen. The guard took a tentative step forward, and his grip tightened on his rifle, raising the barrel a hair. He took another step. Magomed put down his pen and picked up his pistol. Just in case.

A deer exploded from a clump of brambles at the edge of the forest, bounding into the cleared area near the building. The soldier jumped in surprise, quickly raising his rifle to his shoulder and sighting along the tree line where the deer had emerged.

Magomed let out his breath. He chuckled to himself, amused at the scene playing out in front of him.

A second deer burst forth a moment later. The animals froze in place, sniffing at the air, searching for threats. Before Magomed could say a word, the animals sensed the soldier, or maybe Magomed himself. With an almost supernatural grace, they bounded back into the woods. A moment later, it was as if they had never been.

"They always travel in pairs," Magomed called out in his native tongue.

The soldier looked back, seemingly surprised at Magomed's voice. The pale skin of his face had turned a ruddy red with embarrassment.

"Beautiful animals," Magomed continued with a hearty laugh. "But not very bright."

"I'll keep that in mind, sir," the soldier replied. He glanced once again at the forest, then resumed his patrol, hurriedly disappearing around the corner.

Magomed returned to his own work, exchanging his gun for his notebook and pen.

A metal-on-metal shriek tore him from his reverie. *The door.* Footsteps crunched in the pea-sized gravel behind him. He had a visitor.

"This had better be important," he growled, not bothering to look up. Very few people were allowed to interrupt him when he was alone, and only for the most exceptional of reasons.

"We are done," Pytor said, his voice gravelly.

Magomed clicked his pen closed and placed it in his notebook. He spun to face the scientist and sucked in his breath at the exhaustion he saw in Pytor's face. It had been two days since they had last spoken, since the old scientist had sequestered himself in his makeshift laboratory in a nonstop engineering marathon to take the original plutonium pit from the SS-20 warhead, re-machine it into six new cores, and then to integrate each twenty-five kiloton bomb with one of his electronics packages. Magomed's eyes jumped to the miniature radiation dosimeter dangling from Pytor's sweat-stained overalls. The device, the size of a standard business card and as thick as two sticks of chewing gum, was a deep, dark green, like the leaves of the nearby oak tree. *Green is good,* Magomed reminded himself. If Pytor were contaminated, the dosimeter would be yellow, or in the worst case, a bright red. Still, the dark green was a noticeable change from the initial light green, indicating he had been exposed to some not insignificant quantity of radiation, although likely not a life-threatening amount.

Pytor wiped his brow with the back of his sleeve and smiled.

Magomed crossed the space between them in a flash. Unable to contain his excitement, he wrapped his arms around the old man and squeezed until he felt Pytor wince. He took a step back, dropping his hands. "I didn't expect it to go so fast."

A raspy chuckle escaped Pytor's throat. "Neither did I."

"Let's see them!" Magomed reached for the door.

Pytor help up a hand. "There is something I must tell you first—"

Magomed stopped in his tracks. The pained look on Pytor's face said bad news. His hand fell from the door handle. "What is it?"

Pytor took a deep breath. "There were some... troubles... with the separation process."

Magomed cocked his head. "Troubles? How so?"

Pytor gestured at the picnic table. "Please, sit."

Magomed did. Pytor took his place beside him, crossing his spindly legs like a giant spider. Reaching into his breast pocket, he withdrew a pack of Marlboro Reds. He shook one out and replaced the pack. He lit the cigarette and took a deep drag.

The suspense was killing Magomed. He wanted to know what had gone wrong. If Pytor was done, then what was the problem?

"Like I said," Pytor continued. "The separation proved to be more complcx than I originally anticipated. During the process where I took the fragments of the original core and remanufactured them into independent cores, two of the fragments began to heat up—"

"Heat up?" Magomed asked.

"Yes. Heat up. The SS-20 pit is composed of a very pure isotope of plutonium, plutonium 239 to be exact. When exposed to our normal atmosphere, the material has a propensity to spontaneously ignite. Once that happens, the only way to extinguish it is to immerse it in a magnesium oxide mixture." He took another drag on his cigarette, ejecting sinuous streams of blue smoke from his nostrils.

"It caught on fire?" Magomed asked, incredulous. "Why didn't you say something?"

Pytor coughed and flicked his cigarette away

unfinished.

"No. It didn't really catch on fire. But it was close. This was when I was first starting. I had a gas imbalance in the glove box. There was too much oxygen. I managed to secure all of the fragments in a sealed container before the worst of the damage occurred."

Magomed was almost afraid to ask. "What kind of damage?"

Pytor knocked out another cigarette. He rolled it between his fingers, staring at it, not meeting Magomed's eyes. "Extreme pitting."

Out of the corner of his eye, Magomed saw the young guard from earlier round the corner again. He made a shushing motion at Pytor and stood to face the guard. "Give us a few minutes."

The guard didn't ask any questions. He spun on his heel and retreated the way he had come.

"Where were we?" Magomed asked as he took his seat again. "Oh yes. Pitting..."

Pytor tucked his unlit cigarette into his breast pocket. "Yes. Pitting. We lost the two fragments. I examined the damage under a microscope, and it's deeper than our tools can repair."

"So we lost two bombs?"

Pytor sighed and stared at the ground. "Yes. We lost two bombs."

Magomed performed a quick mental calculation. His initial plans had called for Pytor to carve the original warhead into six separate devices. Two were for his own personal use, with the other four intended for sale to raise funds for the next phase of his plans, a return to Chechnya and a bid for the presidency. With only four bombs, he only had two to sell, or three if he were willing to hang the success of his plans on the health of a single device. He needed all six.

"Damn it, Pytor! I need all of them. My plan won't work without six."

Pytor rolled his head, cracking his neck. "I know. Believe me. But there's nothing we can do at this point. The two fragments are not usable as bombs. Not without technology we don't have."

Magomed racked his brain, trying to find a way to reorganize his resources, to make four bombs work. The two bombs he intended to hold back were his hedge against Russian intervention when he made his move in Chechnya. Without the bombs in his back pocket, he couldn't hold off the Russian military machine. The past two wars had proven that.

"Could we package the damaged pits as some kind of radiological bomb?"

Pytor brightened. "We could. It would be difficult. But with another day, I might be able to put something together."

This can work, Magomed thought. *I won't make as much money with dirty bombs, but it should be more than enough to buy my way into power - along with the two working devices.* He grinned, pleased with his ingenuity. "Let's do it."

"Just so you know," Pytor said, "a radiological bomb is much more difficult to shield, more dangerous to transport. Your risk factor goes up significantly."

"How much is *significantly*?"

Pytor considered for a moment. "I recommend you dispose of the radiological bombs as soon as possible. Sell them off to someone you trust, but someone who is not a valuable ally, if you know what I mean."

Magomed did. He had just the person in mind, but not until he took care of a little outstanding business first. "How long?" he asked, excited again.

Pytor yawned. "I need to rest for a few hours." He glanced at his watch. "This time tomorrow, perhaps."

Magomed clapped Pytor on the shoulder. The scientist winced. “I trust your abilities, Pytor. Make it happen, and there’s an additional hundred thousand dollars in it for you.”

Pytor waved him off. “Don’t worry about the money. This was our deal. Six bombs.”

“Even better,” Magomed said, surprised. “I’ll talk to you tomorrow.”

Magomed watched as Pytor unfolded himself from the picnic table and got to his feet. *He can’t keep this pace up much longer*, he thought.

“Tomorrow then,” Pytor said and turned for the door.

“Tomorrow...” Magomed repeated under his breath.

SEVENTEEN

Ottawa International Airport
Midnight

AMANDA LEANED FORWARD AND PEERED through the window as the Gulfstream V came to a stop. It parked somewhere off the main runway complex, in front of an enormous hangar emblazoned with the logo of Holloway Aviation, which was a thinly veiled front company for the Canadian Security Intelligence Service. The tall doors of the hangar were closed, and the structure was dark except for a single yellow bulb blazing over a man-sized door at the left corner of the building. Two black Chevrolet Suburbans rolled around the corner of the far side of the hangar and turned for the plane.

Breathing out, she returned her attention to her immediate surroundings. The stiff plastic zip-ties binding her wrists were cutting off her circulation again, had been since her captors had first bound her in the back of the van outside the hotel. She wriggled her hands for the thousandth time, trying to find a comfortable position.

The man seated beside her gave her a tight smile. “We’re almost there, Ms. Carter. We’ll get rid of those soon.”

Amanda didn’t acknowledge him, instead returning her gaze to their welcoming party. It had been seven years since she had last set foot on Canadian soil. During her absence, she had almost, but not quite, been able to convince herself she didn’t miss her homeland, that her attachment was only a quirk of birth. She had been wrong. Try as she might, she couldn’t ignore the gnawing sense of homesickness bubbling up from deep inside of her, couldn’t shake the feeling that if she had to do it all over again, she would have chosen a different path.

Her troubles had begun during an operation code-named Tantramar Bridge in, of all places, the United States. Amanda was part of a joint task force between the CSIS and the American Central Intelligence Agency, acting as the senior Canadian operative on the American side of the border. The U.S. and Canada were collaborating to intercept suspected Asian terrorist operatives as they traversed the porous border between British Columbia and the U.S. That type of operation was technically under the jurisdiction of the separate countries’ border patrol and law-enforcement agencies, but when rumors of a determined group of Abu Sayyaf extremists—a violent Filipino organization affiliated with Al Qaeda—began cropping up in numerous intelligence data streams, the countries quickly devised a plan to allow the Americans to operate on the Canadian side of the border, while the Canadians did the same on the American side. Built atop an information-sharing regime at the highest levels, Tantramar Bridge allowed a free flow of information in both directions, effectively skirting the legal prohibition against the two intelligence agencies operating within their own borders. It was a stroke of genius, a new paradigm of international sharing that allowed both countries to place seasoned counterterrorist operatives where they were most needed—at home.

For the duration of the operation, Amanda worked from an apartment north of Seattle, in the town of Bellingham. She carried American and Canadian passports, both in different names. Her job was to learn who on the American side was assisting the border crossers and where they went once they entered the country, and then pass the information to her CIA counterparts who would work with the FBI to apprehend the terrorists.

The operation ran for two months without any breaks. Amanda embedded herself into the local community, becoming familiar with both local law enforcement patterns and the local criminal subculture. Being so close to the Canadian border, the inhabitants of that part of the state were accustomed to the multitude of crossers. She quickly learned that, despite the constant warnings from the U.S. government to report suspicious activities, people were more often inclined to keep to themselves, to avoid trouble when possible.

The operation ground on, the pressure from Ottawa and Washington increasing as the weeks dragged by and they made no progress. The only thing that made the operation tolerable was her partner, a Vancouver native named Harry Gayle. Harry was young, at least five years her junior, and hungry for recognition. He had a quick wit, and he wasn't bad on the eyes, either, with his clean-shaven head, linebacker shoulders, and piercing gray eyes. Most days they operated independently, coming together periodically to compare notes and meet with their American counterparts.

Amanda first became suspicious of Harry when he failed to show up for a surveillance operation on an apartment in the north end of town. According to the Americans, the occupant of the apartment was a thirty-one-year-old naturalized citizen with a long history of contributing to online forums sympathetic to Abu Sayyaf. Amanda and Harry had been tasked with breaking into the man's apartment and copying all of the media in his house. They were supposed to make it look as if they had never been there. The target worked the graveyard shift at a twenty-four-hour gas station. He typically left his apartment a little after nine thirty and didn't return until after six in the morning, giving them far more time than they needed to do the job. Amanda estimated they would be in and out in under an hour, unless they ran into encryption. If that were to happen, they were authorized to take the equipment and torch the apartment to cover their tracks.

The day before the operation, Amanda and Harry had agreed to drive separately so they would have two escape routes in case something went wrong. She arrived first, parking halfway down the next block, far enough away to not be noticed, but close enough to confirm their subject had left. She laid her mobile phone on her thigh and waited. Harry was supposed to text her when he arrived.

Nine thirty came and went with no sign of him. She checked her phone, even going so far as to turn it off and back on again. Still no Harry. Amanda debated entering the apartment on her own, but aborted the mission when she received a call from her controller. Earlier in the afternoon, the local police had found the subject in a dumpster behind a Red Lobster, killed via a single gunshot to the head.

Harry showed up the next morning, claiming to have been pulled off on a special assignment. Amanda let it slide. Only a few weeks earlier she herself had been pulled into a special project at the last minute, chasing a potential lead all the way down to Portland.

Several more weeks passed with no progress. Amanda continued to work the local population, keeping her eyes open and her ears to the ground.

The big break came on a Tuesday. She and Harry had been ordered to tail a lone Filipino national who had crossed the border using an identity flagged in the National Terrorist Database. Rather than snatching him at the border, the Americans had allowed him through to see where he went, not unlike a doctor releasing a radioactive dye into a sick patient to track down cancer cells. The subject was traveling on a tourist visa, supposedly visiting relatives in Washington and Oregon.

"You have authorization to use deadly force," her superiors told her, a clear indication the man was no ordinary tourist.

Harry was furious when Amanda informed him of their orders, arguing that the tail was a waste of time, that he had a more important prospect already developed, one he had conveniently failed to mention until that moment.

"Just do it, Harry," she snapped, pulling rank. "That's an order."

Harry switched tactics, turning on the charm, but Amanda would have none of it. She had a job to do, and she was going to do it to the best of her ability. She was tired of Harry and his secretive projects. She wanted him to shut up and take orders, to do the job so they could be done, so she could get the hell out of Washington and return home. *He'll learn*, she thought.

"Come on, Amanda. We're on the ground," Harry

implored. “We know what’s important, and this isn’t it.”

Amanda held firm, reminding him of his responsibility, until finally, he submitted, agreeing to follow her lead. In hindsight, it was obvious. Harry was a facilitator. His job was to ensure the man disappeared into the United States without a trace by drawing attention away from him. He had the access and contacts on both sides of the border. He knew the customs agents, and he knew what the authorities were looking for.

Only their superiors in Ottawa were on to him.

Harry became quiet after their exchange, busying himself with his laptop in the passenger seat of Amanda’s rented white Ford Taurus as she drove across Seattle to the Holiday Inn Express. According to credit card records, the subject had checked in at eight o’clock the previous evening.

Amanda pulled in front of the building and dropped off Harry so he could check with the front desk. When she reached the lobby, he was nowhere to be found. Thinking he had gone to the bathroom, she called his mobile phone. No answer. Once again, Harry was missing in action.

Furious, Amanda stalked down the hallway, heading for the room number given to her by the hotel clerk after she had flashed a set of false FBI credentials. Rounding the corner, she found Harry in a hushed conversation with a small balding Filipino man dressed in tan chinos and a blue oxford shirt. The next moments passed in a blur. The Filipino man saw her first and whispered something to Harry, something she couldn’t hear. Harry spun around, drawing his weapon in one fluid motion and pointing it in her direction.

Too shocked to react, Amanda didn’t have time to draw her own gun. Instead, she ducked into an open hotel room as Harry's first shot plowed into the wall beside her. She fumbled at the small of her back and withdrew her weapon, a compact Glock forty caliber, the same model used by the American FBI. With a quick peek around the corner, she saw Harry, one hand on the shoulder of the much smaller man, the other hand pointing at the exit at the far end of the hallway.

"Harry!" Amanda screamed, leaping into the hallway. "What the hell are you doing?"

Her question was answered with a fusillade of bullets, driving her back into the room for cover. For a brief moment, she considered calling her superiors and asking for support. But that would take too much time. Something was wrong with Harry, something jeopardizing the entire mission. She had to act.

Sucking in her breath, Amanda darted into the hallway and tucked herself behind a door jamb, out of Harry's direct line of fire. She saw the Filipino man racing toward the exit. In her peripheral vision, she spotted a flash of movement behind a housekeeping cart stacked high with towels. *Harry.*

"Come out, Harry! We can talk about this."

Harry fired again. Amanda flinched involuntarily as the bullet rocketed by her head.

She had no choice. Deciding surprise was her best option, she broke cover and charged down the hall, ducking and weaving to present as unpredictable a target as possible. As she got within five feet of the cart, Harry jumped out and, to her surprise, charged straight at her.

Amanda skidded to a stop too late to prevent the collision with her corrupt partner, and they ended up on the floor, a tangle of arms and legs. Her gun slipped from her hand and went skittering across the floor.

Harry rolled on top of her before she could collect

herself, jamming his gun deep into the sensitive flesh of her neck. He scowled. "I told you we should have gone after my other lead. If you hadn't been so damned—"

Amanda's life flashed before her eyes as she scanned her immediate surroundings for something she could use as a weapon. The cart and its contents were too far away.

Harry's eyes narrowed. He was about to shoot. *It's now or never*, she realized. Bucking and twisting with all her might, she drove the point of her knee deep into Harry's crotch. For a moment, it seemed as if the blow had had no effect, but then slowly, inexorably, Harry's grip loosened, and the pressure of the gun against her neck eased.

Amanda tore the gun from Harry's grasp and jammed it into his gut. She squeezed the trigger twice, the roar of the shot muffled by the soft flesh of his belly. Harry hung above her for a second, teetering, his face a mask of shocked disbelief before, after what seemed an eternity, collapsing on top of her, his life blood gushing from the holes in his gut, drenching her, staining her forever. Almost as an afterthought, she turned her head at the distinctive *ker-chunk* of the far-off emergency exit as the Filipino man pushed through and vanished into the bright afternoon sunlight.

~ * * * ~

One of the other CSIS operatives, a trim woman about Amanda's age, moved to the door and wrestled it open, allowing in the moist late-summer Ottawa air. *It's not that different from Washington*, Amanda thought idly as she waited. *Maybe a little cooler...*

Her guard nodded at her, and she got to her feet.

She stretched, rolling her shoulders and standing on her toes so her head brushed against the roof of the cabin. She felt, but didn't see a set of rolling stairs *thump* against the fuselage.

"I guess this is it," she said under her breath as her guard hooked his fingers through the zip-tie on her wrist and began guiding her toward the door.

Putting on her bravest face, Amanda stepped from the plane and onto the rolling stairs. She took her first full breath of Canadian air and suppressed a grim smile.

Home again.

It was time to face her past.

EIGHTEEN

Saint Mary's Church Cemetery
Fairfax, Virginia

KURT SNIFFED AND DRAGGED THE back of his wrist across his cheek, rubbing away a few stray tears that had come up out of nowhere. He dug a crumpled tissue from his back pocket and blew his nose, smashing the soggy remains into a tight ball and returning it to his pocket when he was done.

Today was the first opportunity he had had to visit the graves of his family: his wife Amelia, his daughter Heidi, and the most recent addition to the cemetery, his brother Mike.

The cemetery was a quick hour-and-a-half drive around the Capital Beltway from Annapolis, where he had spent the previous day and a half sequestered with Darlene, working nonstop to jumpstart the new facility and generate some leads. So far, their search had produced more questions than answers. The Marine, Melody Jackson, had definitely been the one to inject the code into the Department of Defense servers, but despite a massive manhunt spanning the entire mid-Atlantic region, there had been no sign of her yet.

In a fit of frustration, Kurt had instructed Darlene to take the afternoon off, to go home and do something, anything to clear her mind, to make room for the patterns he knew were lurking within the bottomless pool of data coursing through her computer. Once she agreed, his thoughts shifted to his own unfinished business. His plan was simple—first a quick trip to the Hertz in Fairfax to return his rental car, then he would to catch a cab to his old house to collect a few changes of clothes, some books for the inevitable down time, and his own car. For the short term, it made far more sense to sleep in naval quarters near their offices than to fight D.C. traffic each day. And besides, the old house was full of memories he wasn't sure he was ready to confront. In hindsight, he guessed that was why he hadn't fought too hard when they had made the decision to set up operations in Maryland instead of Virginia. In the span of a few weeks, Kurt's job had become the sum of his existence, the only thing he thought about day and night. He had always envied his brother in his dedication to his career, his ability and willingness, no, eagerness, to focus on the job at hand. For the first time in his life, Kurt understood what made his brother tick, and the reality was so painfully simple it was almost absurd. The job had become personal. Mike's betrayal and subsequent murder by his own countrymen had burned away the last vestiges of the boy in Kurt and left behind a man.

Once he had his car, Kurt made his way to St. Mary's, located a few miles south from his house. He threaded his way through the picture-perfect manicured grounds, angling toward the rear of the cemetery, the home of the Vetter family plot. His chest grew tighter with each turn, his breath coming in sharp gasps. When he finally reached his destination, he was pleased to discover fresh flowers adorning all three graves, most likely courtesy of his mother. He had considered visiting her after the cemetery, but now that he was there, it didn't seem like such a good idea anymore. She would be full of questions he couldn't answer, questions about his life and admonitions about why he was involved in the same business that had taken her eldest son. He couldn't deal with that type of guilt. Not today.

Kurt dropped to his knees between the graves of his wife and daughter, bracing himself against Amelia's headstone so he wouldn't dissolve into a puddle of despair. The burial mounds had subsided in his absence, showcasing his neglect, which drew a sharp pang of guilt. Parting the bouquet of lilies he had purchased on the way over, he carefully divided the flowers between each grave, counting out each individual stem to ensure the loves of his life received equal shares. When he was done, he withdrew a small carved wooden guinea pig from his pocket, a souvenir from his self-imposed exile in South America, and placed it on Heidi's grave, nestled amongst the fresh-cut flowers. Bowing his head, he allowed his thoughts to drain out, letting the preternatural silence of the cemetery rush in to fill the void.

"I'm sorry I didn't come sooner," he whispered into the still air, his voice laden with contrition. "I..." Another tear escaped his eye and fell to the ground, only to be swallowed up by the uniform blades of close-cropped turf. Deep inside, Kurt knew there was no excuse for not coming sooner, other than his own cowardice, his inability to confront what might have been. He closed his mouth and swallowed his words, their taste a light nothingness as they went back down his throat.

“I promise. I’ll be back soon.” Kissing the tips of his fingers, he touched them first to Amelia’s headstone, and then to Heidi’s, before struggling to his feet and turning to face Mike’s grave.

His burial mound was still fresh, the soil rich, loamy, and teeming with life. Kurt took a step forward. Mike’s death still seemed like something out of a bad dream, something that had happened to someone else. The last time they were together, at his family’s funeral, Mike had been his rock, the one person Kurt could rely upon during the tumultuous events of the day.

“I’ll always be here for you,” Mike had said, standing not far from where he was now interred. Kurt closed his eyes and shook his head, his mind struggling to wrap itself around the enormity of his losses.

“I miss you, Mike.” Kurt choked up and swallowed back the hard lump in his throat, tasting hot salt on his lips as the tears began anew. “It’s not the—”

His phone rang, the sound ripping him from his reverie. For a moment, he considered ignoring it, sending the caller to voicemail without even looking, but in the end, he succumbed, if only to distract himself from the anguish threatening to rip him apart.

“Yeah,” he said, not even looking at the screen.

“Kurt. Dominic here. I wanted to give you a heads up. There’s a chopper leaving in fifteen minutes. You need to be on it.”

Kurt turned away from the graves, pressing the phone against his ear so hard it hurt. “I’m off the clock now, Dom.”

Dominic took a deep breath. “Not anymore. Helen Bartholomew, one of the agency people involved in the incident with your brother, is asking for you."

Kurt's mind lurched. Helen was the only living link to Mike. She alone could tell him what had happened to him, how he had come to fall so far. "Did she say why?"

"No. All I know is she asked for you. Insisted, actually."

"Insisted?"

"Yes."

Turning, Kurt let his gaze drift over the tree line at the far end of the cemetery.

"Are you still there?" Dominic asked.

Kurt blinked. "Yeah. I'm here. Where is she?"

"She's at an agency detention facility in Winchester. Don't worry. The helicopter will take you there and bring you back."

"I'm in Fairfax right now, visiting my family."

Dominic was silent for a moment. "I'm sorry to interrupt."

"Don't worry about it." Kurt turned toward his car. "I was almost done."

"Okay. I'll have the chopper meet you at Langley. Darlene's already in the air. Call me as soon as you're finished." Dominic ended the call.

A warm breeze came up out of nowhere, pushing through the cemetery like an invisible tsunami. The leaves on the trees around Kurt rustled for a moment, and then became still again as the breeze passed.

With a final longing glance at what remained of his family, Kurt climbed into his car and turned the key.

NINETEEN

Nashville, Tennessee
Midnight

GREG SAT IN HIS CAR with the engine running, pondering the wisdom of what he was about to do. He had been on the road for a little over eleven hours, driving straight from Washington to Nashville, stopping only for gas and an artery-clogging burger and fries at a Hardee's somewhere off Interstate 81 in southwest Virginia. A mostly empty carton of Camel Lights sat on the passenger seat. He had been chain-smoking the entire drive, lighting each succeeding cigarette from the butt of the previous. Every breath he took began and ended with a wheezing rattle. The successive layers of tar and nicotine had obliterated his sense of taste and smell, leaving his nose clogged with great balls of rocky snot, and his tongue feeling as though he had licked the ass of a comatose vagrant in Dupont Circle. He knocked a cigarette from a box on the dashboard and lit up, greedily sucking down the smoke. Two years cigarette-free were down the drain.

He didn't care. Not anymore. His life was fucked beyond repair. Viktor had taken his software and done something with it, something that triggered an evacuation of the White House and pandemonium in Washington only rivaled by the events of 9/11. Try as he might, Greg couldn't figure out how his software could have caused that. When Viktor had delivered the first code bundle to him, he immediately assumed it did something illegal. It was Viktor, after all. He didn't have to make very many changes to the first batch, minor modifications to correct some compilation errors that the previous programmer had introduced. He made the fixes and turned it around in under a day. The next code drop was far more voluminous. Still, standing alone, Greg wasn't sure of its function. He had asked Viktor, of course, but Viktor was vague in his description. That had been enough for Greg at the time. He didn't really care what the software did, only that it got Viktor off of his back, helped him erase his debt. He would write software all day long if it helped him get out from under, if it helped him stay alive.

Greg's car shuddered as the electric motor cut out. Idling his Prius meant it would constantly switch back and forth between gasoline and electric power. The motor kicked in again. The blasting air conditioner was proving too much for the batteries. He glanced at the temperature display in the center console. Eighty-seven degrees. He cursed under his breath. Of all the places to live...

Jenny Cooper, his former girlfriend, lived on the top floor of the apartment building directly across the street. Light blazed from her windows, a clear indication she was still awake. Greg smiled as he thought of their time together. Like him, Jenny was a night owl, often staying up until the early hours of the morning, chatting on internet message boards and playing video games with other similarly addicted people scattered across the globe. Ironically, it had been her inability to turn off her computer addiction and focus on the real world that had caused the demise of their relationship a year earlier. At least, that was what he told himself. Their breakup, while sudden in Greg's opinion, had been amicable. When she announced three months earlier she was leaving the D.C. area and moving to Nashville, he wished her well and told her to stay in touch. They had exchanged several emails since then, but had not spoken on the phone.

Greg sucked down the last of his cigarette, then pushed the electric window button to lower the window a crack. He shoved the spent butt through the gap and watched it tumble out of sight. His fingers came back in moist, wet from the soupy Nashville summer evening. He shuddered at the thought of entering the steam bath. *It can't be worse than Washington*, he thought.

He pushed the power button, and the car turned off. Screwing up his courage, he climbed out and set out across the street.

Two minutes later, he knocked on her front door. He heard footsteps from within and Jenny's familiar voice as she yelled for him to wait. The sound brought a sad smile to his face. He waited patiently as she looked at him through the peephole. The door shook in its frame, and the deadbolt clattered as Jenny unlocked it.

She stared at him, her eyes narrowed. "Greg?"

"Hi, Jenny."

A male voice called out from somewhere inside the apartment. "Is everything okay out there, Jen?"

Jenny hissed, "What are you doing here? This is

not a good time." She glanced over her shoulder.

The door opened wider, and a man appeared behind her. He was about Greg's build, but while Greg was clean-shaven with sandy-blond hair, the other man was bald and sported a goatee. *A musician,* Greg thought.

"I'm sorry," Greg said, taking a step back. "I didn't mean to interrupt. I can come back later."

Jenny shook her head. "Paul," she said, putting her hand on the other man's shoulder. "This is Greg, my ex-boyfriend. Greg, this is Paul."

The men tentatively shook hands.

"You may as well come in," Jenny said, stepping aside.

"Thanks," Greg said, trying to ignore the suspicious glare coming from Paul.

Together, they moved to the small living room, which was packed with computer equipment, video game consoles, and flat-screen televisions. Paul picked up an open laptop from a recliner, snapped the lid closed, and placed it on top of a speaker. "Sorry for the mess," he said with a shrug. "I've been meaning to clean." He joined Jenny on the couch.

Jenny looked Greg up and down. "I don't want to sound mean, Greg, but you look like shit. And what's with the smoking? I thought you quit."

Greg ran his fingers through his hair, and his palm came away greasy. He looked at his chest and noticed a teardrop-shaped blob of dried ketchup over his sternum. "It's a long story," he replied obliquely. "Really long."

Paul stood. He looked nervous. "Can I get you guys something to drink while you catch up?"

"No, thanks," Jenny said.

Greg considered the offer a second before shaking his head. "I'm good."

"I'll be back." Paul headed down the hall toward what Greg assumed was the kitchen.

Jenny leaned forward on the couch. "I can't believe you just showed up here. Are you in town for business or something?"

Greg shook his head. "No. I came straight from D.C."

Jenny looked surprised. "D.C.? You drove here?"

Greg coughed into his hand, a harsh, lung-rattling explosion. "You know," he said as he came up for air, "maybe I will take a glass of water."

Jenny turned toward the hall. "Paul! Can you bring Greg some water?"

"Thanks," Greg murmured. "I know this is awkward..."

Jenny waved her hand at him. "Paul's cool. We had lunch with his ex only last week. Don't worry."

Greg relaxed a fraction. He wondered how cool Paul would be after he asked Jenny his next question.

"So, what's going on?" Jenny asked. "What in the world brings you here of all places?"

At that moment, Paul returned and handed Greg a half-liter bottle of Arrowhead water. He had put on a shirt with *West Virginia University* emblazoned across the chest.

"They had a good season last year," Greg commented, nodding at Paul's shirt.

Paul looked down and smiled. "Yeah. We're still building." He put a hand on Jenny's shoulder, leaned over, and kissed her on the forehead. "I'm heading off to bed. I'll see you in a while..."

Jenny drew him in and kissed him on the mouth, no doubt embellishing the act for Paul's benefit. "I'll be in soon."

"Good night, Greg," Paul said. "Don't keep her up too long."

"Good night, Paul. And thanks."

With a quick nod, Paul turned and set off down the hall, leaving Greg and Jenny alone.

Greg waited until Paul was out of earshot before continuing. "Look. There's a lot going on, a lot I want to tell you, but right now, I'm beat to shit. I'm wired to the teeth on caffeine and nicotine, but I can feel my body screaming at me for sleep. I've got a huge favor to ask, but I'll understand if you say no."

Jenny tensed, and Greg knew right away that she had guessed what he was going to ask. He went ahead. "Can I crash with you guys for a few nights? I'll explain more in the morning, after I've had time to sort through it all."

Jenny put her head in her hands, her long blond hair falling over and hiding her face. Greg knew the position. It was her response to an overwhelming situation. He also knew that his best course of action was to let her work through it, rather than to push her.

"Paul won't like it," she said from behind her curtain of hair. "But..."

Greg waited.

She looked up at him. He saw tears in the corners of her eyes, tiny droplets that hadn't yet succumbed to gravity. "Sure." She said it again with more conviction, and then got to her feet.

Greg stood as well. "Thank you, Jenny. You have no idea—"

She ignored him and pointed down the hall. "Towels and blankets are in the closet on your right. You can sleep on the couch. I'll break the news to Paul..."

"Great!" Greg said. "I'll go get my stuff."

Jenny gave him a forced smile. "Only for a couple of days. Then you have to move on. I've got something good with Paul, and I don't want to screw it up. I really don't."

"I understand," Greg said, meaning it. Getting back with Jenny was the farthest thing from his mind at the moment. All he could think of was staying as far away as possible from Viktor.

"Goodnight, Greg," Jenny said, her gaze full of a mix of pity and sadness that made Greg die a little inside. "We'll talk more in the morning."

"Yes. Goodnight. And Jenny?"

She stopped.

"Thanks again. I mean it."

"It's okay, Greg. I'm glad to help."

She turned and headed to her bedroom.

TWENTY

CIA Operation Center
Winchester, Virginia

"I'VE NEVER HEARD OF THIS place," Kurt muttered as he and Darlene strode down the hall in the bowels of the secret rural CIA detention facility. Their escort, who had identified himself only as Branson, wore no uniform, no insignia, yet he carried himself with the bearing of a man accustomed to being in charge of others.

Darlene shot Kurt an annoyed glance and said nothing. She picked up her pace, pulling a few steps ahead of him. Kurt got the message. Sometimes it was better not to ask questions.

They had arrived by helicopter fifteen minutes earlier, touching down on the roof of the facility located seventy miles west of Washington, near the West Virginia border. From the outside, there was no indication of the building's true purpose. It could have been the headquarters of an insurance company, for all Kurt could tell. Inside was a different story altogether.

Once they passed through the single reinforced steel door on the roof, Branson stopped them at a heavily armored guard shack and instructed them to place all weapons and recording devices into a plastic tray, similar to those used at the airport. They complied, although Darlene made it clear she was upset about leaving her phone behind. The guard took their belongings and then buzzed them through another heavy door. From there, they boarded an elevator for the short ride down to the fourth floor.

They arrived at the last door at the end of the hall, and Branson motioned for them to stop. “She’s in here,” he said, gesturing at the nondescript wooden door.

“Is she alone?” Darlene asked.

Branson grunted an affirmative.

Kurt moved toward the door. “Is there anything we should know? Anything special?”

Branson shook his head. “Only that she hasn’t said a word until now.”

“This is being recorded, I assume?” Darlene asked.

Branson showed his teeth. “Of course. We’ll have eyes and ears on the entire exchange.”

“Good. I’ll need the recordings afterward.”

Branson nodded. “Not a problem.”

“Let’s do this,” Kurt said. He knocked once and pushed into the room. Helen sat at a small metal table, facing the door. An empty plastic chair was stationed across from her, its arms tucked under the edge of the table. To his surprise, she wasn’t restrained. She appeared relaxed, at ease with her situation. A twenty-ounce bottle of Diet Coke rested by her right hand.

She got to her feet and extended her hand. “I didn’t expect you so soon.”

Kurt put his hands in his pockets. "It sounded important."

Helen returned to her seat, ignoring his snub. "Please. Sit."

"I'd rather not."

Helen shrugged. "Suit yourself." She unscrewed the cap on her drink and took a sip, then replaced the cap.

Kurt placed his hands on the back of the chair. "So, what do you have for me?"

"You look like your brother," Helen said softly. "Has anyone ever told you that?"

That caught Kurt off guard. He tried to play it off. "Sure. Plenty of times."

Helen shook her head. "It's just… it kind of surprised me, the resemblance. Are you sure you don't want to sit? It may be better if you do."

Kurt pulled out the chair and took a seat. "Happy?"

"Yeah. That's better." Helen worried at the plastic label on the soda bottle. "Look, I want to start off by saying I'm sorry about your brother. He was one of the good guys." Her eyes flitted away from him for a moment, as if she were somehow embarrassed to be under his scrutiny.

Kurt took a deep breath, wondering where that had come from. According to the briefing materials he had read on the way in, Helen had worked with Mike, but the details of her role had been heavily redacted, blacked out by the CIA censors. He was operating from a distinct disadvantage.

"Thanks," he muttered. "We all miss him." He forced himself to soften up, to let her talk, to get whatever she had to say off her chest. "So, why the sudden desire to talk? Why now? And why me?"

Helen shifted in her chair, then met his eyes. "Look. I fucked up. Big time. I'm not going to argue about that. I doubt I'll ever see the light of day again." She paused for a moment and stared into her lap. "But that's my problem. Not yours."

Kurt said nothing, waiting.

Helen met his eyes again. "We thought we were doing the right thing, setting the bomb in Moscow. But it all fell apart so fast. When your brother bolted with the data, we didn't have a choice. We had to stop—"

Kurt's vision dimmed as Helen spoke. All of the myriad details from her dossier clicked into place, her role in the operation, the reason she had summoned him, all of it.

"Were you there?" he demanded, gripping the edges of the table until his knuckles turned white.

Helen shook her head vigorously. "No. Oh, no. I wasn't there when—"

"When he was killed."

"Yes. When he was killed."

"Who then?"

"That's not important."

It took everything in Kurt's power to retain his composure. He wanted to leap across the table and strangle the pathetic woman, wanted to choke the life out of her, to make her pay for what she had done to his brother, to his family.

"So you think confessing to me makes everything all right?" he asked, the fury popping and bubbling through the thin veneer of his voice.

Helen turned red. "No. Nothing I can say will make this right."

"You're goddamned right it won't!" Kurt leapt to his feet and wrenched the table aside. Losing all control, he took two steps forward and grabbed Helen by the shoulders, shaking her with all his might. "You selfish bitch! You took my brother away from me! Do you have any idea what you did?"

Hot tears spattered on his hand. It took Kurt a moment to realize they were his own.

Then, as soon as it had appeared, his rage was gone. Kurt became acutely aware of what he was about to do, of how close he had come to throwing away everything he believed. Instantly disgusted with himself, he released her and took a step back. The world snapped into focus, and he glanced around, searching for the hidden recording devices, acutely embarrassed at his outburst, ashamed at losing control.

Helen sobbed, slumped in her chair, a faint shadow of the confident woman who had greeted him.

Kurt collected himself and righted the table. Squeezing his fists repeatedly to suppress the remnants of his anger, he returned to his seat. Helen would be punished for her crimes. Her entire confession had been caught on tape. Any doubts as to her role were now dispelled.

"Is that it?" he asked, once his breathing returned to normal. "Is that everything?"

"No," Helen said. "There's more."

"There always is."

"It's not over."

"What do you mean?"

Helen winced. "You blew the top off of our plans, you shut us down, and you made it look easy. You're a bona fide hero now."

Kurt hadn't thought of his actions in Moscow in that light, and he wasn't sure he was comfortable with Helen's choice of words. Given a choice, he would have given it all up in a heartbeat if it meant bringing back his brother. "I don't know about that," he said cautiously.

Helen's chair screeched as she pulled it closer to the table. "Well, I do. And if you've got that kind of power, you need to use it, because it won't last. I wanted you dead two weeks ago. I tried my best to eliminate you, but you have to understand I was only doing my job. But now, given the circumstances, I have information that may help, may let you unwind the mess I created."

Kurt grimaced. Helen's personnel records were rife with comments about her dedication to her job, her undying loyalty to the CIA, and especially her former boss. Try as he might, he couldn't help but feel a twinge of sympathy. She had gotten wrapped up with the wrong group of people, seduced by a broken ideology, and she was trying to undo the damage she had inflicted upon the country.

"Go on..."

Helen spoke for almost an hour. Fifteen minutes in, Kurt told her to pause for a minute while he stepped out of the room and requested paper and a pen with which to take his own notes. Her story deviated significantly from the official version he had received. Starting with a bold scheme hatched by her former boss, whom Kurt had met briefly at his brother's wake, she recounted her version of the plot to engage a disgruntled Chechen warlord to detonate a nuclear device in Moscow. Her words filled in many of the gaps in the official version, while also introducing countless new and disturbing questions. Some of those Kurt attributed to need-to-know, some to pure disinformation, both from Helen and the government. The final piece in her puzzle was a theory so far-fetched, yet aligning so closely with current events that Kurt had no choice but to consider its veracity. According to Helen, the CIA had been double-crossed by the Chechen; the bomb in Moscow was nothing but a ruse, a dummy warhead intended to throw both the Russians and the Americans into disarray while the

Chechen spirited away the real device for his own purposes. The Russians, she claimed, knew that and were withholding the information to buy time while they searched for the missing bomb.

Darlene was waiting in the hall when Kurt exited the interrogation room. Branson was gone.

“So…” Darlene said, clearly uncomfortable.

“Did you catch all of that?” Kurt said.

Darlene nodded. “I did. Are you okay?” she asked, referring, he assumed, to his outburst.

“I think so.” He took a deep breath. “Her story… it sounds almost too insane to believe, but I think there’s a kernel of truth in there.”

“I think so, too.”

“Come on.” Kurt set off down the hall at a fast walk. “We have a lot of work to do.”

TWENTY-ONE

CSIS Headquarters
Interrogation Room 3A
Ottawa, Canada

AMANDA STARED AT THE DOCUMENT lying on the table before her, barely registering the voice in the background droning on about culpability and repercussions. She had been in the four-by-five meter interrogation room for six hours and had long ago passed the point where she gave a damn how long they kept her. She wasn't going to sign the confession.

The document, a single page covered with dense text on both sides, had a space for her signature, as well as her interrogators, at the bottom of each side. Its very existence represented everything about her old life that she had tried so hard to escape. The bureaucracy, the inane rules, the sheer self-importance of the people buzzing about the CSIS headquarters, she detested all of it.

She yawned and wondered how Kurt was doing. Any thoughts of a phone call to her attorney or loved one were a sad joke. She was at the bottom of a deep, dark well, a non-person, her mere existence subject to the whims of the Canadian government.

"Ms. Carter." Her interrogator snapped his fingers in front of her face. "Please pay attention. This is important."

Amanda gave him a wan smile and slid the paper back across the table. For the fourth time. Each interrogator had tried a different angle. The first, a young East Indian man with a singsong voice and the richest toffee complexion she had ever seen had come in acting as if they were long lost friends. Full of promises of understanding and cooperation, he had spent twenty-five long minutes talking before sliding the page to her. In character with the conversation, Amanda had politely declined, turning the paper around, and pushing it back with a polite smile.

Next up was a woman, closer to her age. Amanda thought she looked familiar when she first entered, but as soon as the woman opened her mouth, she realized she had been mistaken. That interrogator had played the part of the bad cop, reversing all of the offers the previous interrogator had presented, enumerating the penalties for the crimes she had supposedly committed in great detail. She had even gone so far as to threaten Amanda with life in prison in the Northwest Territories, where she would either die of cold or be carried off by one of the carnivorous mosquitoes that emerged from the tundra each spring.

Amanda had declined. She didn't bother asking for an attorney. None would be provided. She had signed away that right many years ago upon first entering the CSIS. According to the oath she had taken, they owned her, down to the last molecule of her being.

That they hadn't gone to the United Kingdom and taken her home forcibly was a testament to the elaborate safeguards Amanda had instituted so many years ago. When she first set up her safe-house, she approached it with the knowledge that blackmailing the British and Canadian governments, threatening them with a data disclosure that would make WikiLeaks look like child's play, was a fantastic gamble. But it had paid off. Her old friend Nigel Hawthorne, now dead at the hand of a rogue CIA assassin, had proven instrumental in formulating her dead man's switch, a mechanism whereby an extensive cache of encrypted content, handpicked by herself and Nigel, would be automatically decrypted and delivered to the major world media organizations in the event of her untimely death. The idea wasn't new, only the scope. Or the *supposed* scope. In truth, Amanda never had any incriminating data on the U.K. or Canadian governments. It was all a bluff, a ruse calculated to instill fear into a security and political apparatus terrified of the next big leak. Despite her desire to remain immune from extradition, her allegiance to the safety of the other men and women working undercover around the world, regardless of whether they worked for the United Kingdom, the Canadians, or the Americans, was paramount. She would never have done anything to jeopardize their safety. They had tested her, both the Canadians and the British. On Nigel's recommendation, she had released a small bundle of marginally interesting intelligence data, top-secret diplomatic chatter long past its expiration date, nothing that would threaten the safety of operatives in the field. When the British pressed, she allowed a day to pass without a text message from her mobile phone to her secure server in Singapore, and two hundred pages of documents were emailed to the head of MI-6 and the Canadian prime minister.

The next day, the van parked outside her house was gone.

But that was then. There she was, back in Canada, at the mercy of the CSIS. Her plan had backfired. Something had changed, something she couldn't have foreseen. And for the life of her, she couldn't figure out what it was.

She met the interrogator's eyes and let a long sigh escape. "For the last time, I'm not signing anything."

The man, somewhere on the downward slope of middle age, with a fast-receding hairline and a square jaw gone soft, traced his index finger in a tight figure eight on the scuffed metal table, seemingly deep in thought. Amanda waited.

His finger stopped. "In that case, I think we're done for now."

Amanda stretched and cracked her knuckles. She knew they weren't really done. No. They were only getting started. "Good. I'd like to visit the restroom then."

The man ignored her as he stood and retrieved the paper and pen. The pen went into his breast pocket. The paper went into a manila folder with yellow bars of tape across the top.

"Hey, I said I need to go to the bathroom." She really did have to pee. It had been two hours and three cups of coffee since her last break.

He stopped for a moment, regarding her as if seeing her for the first time. Then, with a disgusted shake of his head, he turned and left the room. The door snapped shut behind him with a solid *click*.

Amanda shuffled her feet, or tried to as the bolt holding her ankle shackles didn't allow for much movement. Her ass tingled from remaining seated for so long. The shackles were overkill—interrogation theater, there for the sole purpose of intimidating her.

It was too bad she wasn't easily intimidated. They had trained her, after all.

A minute passed. And then another. Finally, she heard the regular *clip-clop* of heavy footsteps in the hall. The person stopped outside her door. A moment later, the door swung open, and another man entered.

Amanda did a double take. Standing in front of her was her former supervisor, Maxwell Riggs.

"Max?"

"Amanda." He closed the door.

Max, she noticed, carried the same folder as her previous interrogator. "Mind if I sit?"

Amanda gestured at the empty chair across from her. "Be my guest." She stole a glance at the badge hanging from his breast pocket. "Director Riggs," she said with mock awe. "You've moved up in the world."

Max blushed and looked her in the eye. "You've been gone a long time, Amanda. Things change. People change."

"They sure do. But not you. You still look good. You always did."

His only acknowledgment was an almost imperceptible nod. "You know this is serious, don't you? We know all about the fake data. I have to admit, that was a ballsy move. And I... no, *we* do appreciate your discretion."

Amanda rolled her eyes. "Did you really think I would do anything to risk the people here?"

Max shrugged. "It sure looked like it at the time. Oh, by the way, you owe the government a little over two million dollars for your little stunt with the encryption. Resources, you know. Computer people. Mathematicians. The works."

Amanda shot him a sardonic smile. "Put it on my tab."

Max leaned back in his chair and tugged at his tie.

"This would be so much easier if you just signed the paperwork."

Amanda bent forward, placing her hands on the sides of the table and getting within spitting distance of her former supervisor. "You still don't get it, do you, Max? I didn't do it. I had nothing to do with Harry and his little side operation. It was as much a surprise to me as it was to you."

Max shook his head. "I wish I could believe you. I really do. But you know the evidence. Hell, you've seen it, most of it at least. And running like you did…"

He was right. She *had* seen the evidence. Emails, text messages, and maps, all collected from Harry's house during the course of the investigation. That Harry had been so sloppy with his information management was in itself almost criminal. The fact that it was all fabricated, an elaborate trap constructed to shift blame from himself to her, still made her wonder how he had pulled it off. Or why. Actually, she knew the why. Harry must have realized he couldn't stay one step ahead of the CSIS and the CIA forever. Being young and ambitious, he had an exit plan lined up. That was what she would have done. Unfortunately, no one had believed her. It was her word against the word of a dead man with good family connections.

"You have to believe me, Max," she said, a pleading edge creeping into her voice. "I had nothing to do with it."

"Excuse me." Max reached into his pocket and pulled out his phone. He frowned. "I'm sorry, but I have to take this. We'll continue tomorrow."

"But—"

Max was already up and out of his chair, heading for the door. A moment later, he was gone.

Amanda sat alone in silence, digesting the new

turn of events. Max had always liked her. At one point, she had suspected he had a crush on her, but being the consummate professional, he had never acted on it. Or it could have been her imagination. *Whatever.* It didn't matter anymore. With Max involved, for the first time, Amanda felt she might have a chance of escaping the walls before they closed in on her completely.

The door swung open again. Her regular guards entered the room. "We're done for the afternoon, Ms. Carter," the short one said. His partner, six inches taller and one hundred pounds heavier, observed in silence. Amanda didn't think he had much going on up top.

"I was wondering when I'd see you guys again," she said sarcastically. "I don't know where you get these interrogators, but none of them seem to understand that when a woman says no, she means no."

Her weak joke drew a rare smile from the larger guard. He bent to one knee and unlocked her leg shackles as the other guard circled around behind her.

"So what's next?" she asked as they helped her to her feet.

Five minutes later, she was back in her cell, alone for the first time all day. Darkness had come and stolen another day in her absence, leaving only a small sliver of black sky and a faint scattering of stars to remind her of the world outside.

Amanda began to cry.

~ * * * ~

Dominic took a quick sip of his coffee and licked his lips. "Look, Max," he said into his phone. "I understand your position. I've been there myself."

"In that case—" Riggs started.

"Hold on. I said I understand. I didn't say I agree."

He pressed on before Riggs could put up an argument. "Think about how it would look for Canada if the media learned you had abducted a U.S. citizen in broad daylight, snatched her from her hotel in Washington, and put her on a plane against her will. That's not the kind of image Canada wants. Is it?"

"Now, hold on just a minute," Riggs said, the indignation palpable in his voice.

"No," Dominic said sharply. "I'm tired of talking about this. You abducted an American citizen. We want her back, and we want her now."

"You wouldn't do that," Riggs said.

Dominic smiled. Under normal circumstances, Riggs was correct. On any other day, the negotiation would have been managed through diplomatic channels, and he wouldn't have had to resort to open threats. But it wasn't a normal situation. "Try me."

Riggs didn't speak right away. His breathing had changed, Dominic noticed. Shallower. Faster.

"I need to speak with some people," Riggs said finally.

"You do that," Dominic said. "I understand you're quite the rising star in the CSIS. I'd hate to be the one to end your career."

"What's that supposed to mean?"

"Think about it. I'll look forward to hearing from you."

Dominic hung up the phone and leaned back in his chair. He had never before gone so far out on a limb with a major ally. He didn't know if Riggs would believe him, if he would fall for his outrageous bluff, and he didn't have anything else in his back pocket if he didn't. Since Amanda was technically a citizen of both countries, Canada was well within its legal rights to prosecute her for whatever crimes she had committed. Going public would not only end Max

Riggs' career, it would also end Dominic's.

His ploy had to work. Otherwise, Amanda could be lost to the United States forever.

TWENTY-TWO

CIA Operation Center
Winchester, Virginia

KURT AND DARLENE COLLECTED THEIR belongings from the guard shack and headed for the exit. Kurt could already hear the roar of the helicopter preparing for their departure.

He put his hand on the door to push it open, but stopped short when he got an idea. The interrogation had given him a new perspective on their mission and, instead of having his questions answered, he had more of them. What Helen had told him contradicted everything he thought he knew. According to the officials he had spoken with since his return, the bomb had been an isolated device, and the Russians had taken care of it. He thought back to the team of Spetsnaz soldiers storming the warehouse, trying to recall their behavior. Had there been any indication they hadn't found what they were expecting? He couldn't recall. He wished Amanda was with him so he could ask her. She always seemed more tuned in to that sort of thing, more perceptive of her surroundings.

He held up an open hand to Darlene. “Hold on. Change of plans.”

“What’s up?” she asked with a raised eyebrow.

“I’m going to make a stop on the way back, check in with Dominic and brief him on Helen’s story. I want you to head back without me. Start digging, and see how much of it is true. I’ve got a bad feeling…”

“Are you sure you don’t want backup?”

Kurt shook his head. “No. It’s better that I go by myself.”

Darlene gave him a dubious look but didn’t protest.

A few minutes later, they roared east into the coming darkness.

TWENTY-THREE

The White House
Office of the National Security Advisor

"MR. VELASQUEZ WILL SEE YOU now," Dominic's assistant announced from her desk across the room. She got up and made her way to Dominic's office. She put her hand on the lever and waited for Kurt to approach before opening the door.

Kurt grimaced at the formality. He had called Dominic from his car to let him know he was on the way, and at the time, Dominic had made it abundantly clear there would be no delays. Why then, Kurt wondered, had he been made to sit in the lobby for a full ten minutes before being granted access? His mind roiled with a stew of conspiracy theories, and the unexpected behavior, along with Helen's revelations, fed them with abandon.

"Thank you," he said as he passed.

"Kurt, come in! Have a seat," Dominic said, waving from behind his desk.

Kurt couldn't help but notice the bags under Dominic's eyes, the tie loosened at his throat, and the rolled-up sleeves. On every other occasion Kurt had spoken to Dominic in person, even in the helicopter during the evacuation from the White House, the man had seemed calm and composed, an unflappable example of a confident executive who didn't let the stress of the job get to him. Today, Dominic looked as if he had just run a marathon.

"Thanks for seeing me," Kurt said as he slid into a wingback chair across from Dominic.

"Sorry for the wait. I was in the middle of something."

Kurt waited for him to elaborate, but nothing more seemed forthcoming. "Not a problem. It's important, but not urgent. At least, I don't think it is yet."

"So what have you got? What did Helen have to say?"

Kurt suppressed a scowl. "That's actually why I came here instead of calling."

Dominic picked up an engraved gold ballpoint pen from his desk and twirled it in his fingers slowly, going first from one side of his hand to the other and then back again. "Well, let's hear it."

Kurt spent the next several minutes recapping his meeting with Helen, starting with her contrition over her involvement in the failed plot and moving quickly into her assertions regarding the Russians and the missing bomb. He concluded by describing his impressions of her body language and voice tone as she relayed her story. Kurt tried to couch his suspicions about the lack of honesty on the President and Dominic's part in the most diplomatic language possible. Dominic listened patiently, nodding whenever Kurt made an important point and even taking a few notes along the way.

"What I need to know is," Kurt said, "do you believe there is any reason I should give weight to her accusations? When President Cooper asked me to do this job, he told me I had all the resources of the government at my disposal. I assumed that meant intelligence, but it seems that may not be the case at all. I can't do this job if you're holding back information."

Dominic gave Kurt a wry grin. "You have a good memory."

That caught Kurt off guard. "What do you mean?"

In response, Dominic extracted a folder from his top drawer and slid it across his desk. Opening it, Kurt discovered a transcript of the conversation between himself and Helen.

"What's this?" he demanded, his temper flaring. "If you knew what we talked about, then why didn't you say so? Why'd you let me ramble on like that?"

Dominic placed his pen on the edge of his blotter and pushed his chair back. He undid his tie the rest of the way, pulled it off, and laid it carefully on his desk. "It's a long story."

Kurt stole a glance at the clock on the far wall. "I've got time."

"She's telling the truth," Dominic said. "At least, we think she is. We began to suspect something was wrong even before you and Amanda returned from Moscow. If you recall from your debriefing, the bomb in question came from a joint program between us and the Russians, set up when the wall fell. Once the fireworks in Moscow died down, we requested an on-site inspection of the fissile material, and were denied. We even sent a special team of engineers over to analyze the device to ensure it was in a safe condition, but the Russians turned them away at the gate."

Kurt couldn't believe what he was hearing. "And

when were you going to tell me this?"

Dominic shrugged. "Soon. The State Department has been leaning on the Russians for the past week, trying to get them to say something, anything, but so far, they've ignored every request."

Kurt leaned back in his chair and ran his fingers through his hair. "I can't believe this. Not only do we have a hacker in the DoD network, but the bomb Amanda and I risked our lives to stop doesn't even exist."

Dominic gave him a grave nod. "That about sums it up. I'm sorry I couldn't tell you the truth earlier. We had our reasons. You've got to understand."

Oddly enough, Kurt did. That was how things worked in Washington. Sometimes it was like peeling layers from a rotten onion, complexity wrapped within complexity.

He stood and took a step toward Dominic's desk. "If you want me to do this job, you can't hold anything back. If that's not possible, then I'd like to tender my resignation. Right now."

Dominic got to his feet and crossed his arms across his chest. "No. That won't be necessary. I agree with you one hundred percent. From this point on, no more secrets." He held out his hand. "Deal?"

Kurt surveyed him for a long moment before finally extending his own hand. It was the best he was going to get. "Deal."

The issue settled for the moment, both men returned to their seats.

Dominic spoke first. "What next?"

Kurt settled in his chair. "I've got Darlene taking another pass through the CIA records. She'll find something now that we have a few names to work with."

"And if she doesn't?"

"She will," Kurt said with grim determination. "She will."

TWENTY-FOUR

Outside of Cluj, Romania

"I CAN BARELY TELL THE difference," Magomed said with a hint of awe in his voice. He knelt down and ran his hand along the ground, scooping up a handful of loose dirt and letting it sift through his fingers in thin, crumbly streams. "It's all buried?"

Pytor nodded. "Yes. I personally tested the workshop and all of the equipment we used to bury the manufacturing tools. None of the radiation readings exceed normal background levels."

Magomed got to his feet and held out his hand. "Do you mind?"

"Not at all." Pytor gave him a Geiger counter, a small box roughly the size of a large mobile phone. "Push the button at the top."

Magomed pushed the button and began tracing the perimeter of the half-filled-in pit. His eyes remained glued to the display the entire time. While he inspected, Pytor stood off to the side, smoking. Once Magomed finished measuring the pit, he strolled over to the rusting yellow Caterpillar backhoe parked a few meters away. He circled the construction equipment, paying particular attention to the treads and to the bucket.

"It's clean," he announced a minute later. He returned the Geiger counter to Pytor. "How deep did you go?"

"Four meters. It is enough."

Magomed raised an eyebrow. "If you say so. And the bombs?"

Pytor motioned at the workshop on the far side of the tree line. "They're in there, packed and waiting."

"And the men?" Magomed asked with no small amount of dread.

Pytor coughed once and flicked his dead cigarette into the dirt. "Only two men were close enough to the equipment to see it, and I don't think they understood."

Magomed scratched his chin. "Good." He pulled a portable radio from his pocket and held it to his mouth, holding down the transmit button with his thumb. "Mansur. Round up the men and meet in the garage."

"Yes, sir." Mansur Bargishev had worked with Pytor to bury the equipment, and he was the most knowledgeable about the events in the ex-Soviet facility. He was one of Magomed's most trusted men, having fought side by side with him in both wars against the Russians. Magomed would be sorry to lose him, but it was a necessity.

His plan was about to enter the third, and arguably, most dangerous phase. Phase one had been procuring the raw nuclear material. For the second phase, he had relied upon a core group of six soldiers, Mansur included, as well as a group of a dozen mercenaries to whom he felt no allegiance. Most of the mercenaries had died in the firefight with the

Americans and the Russian *Spetsnaz* troops in Moscow, tools used and discarded once their purpose was exhausted. The remaining men, however, had a much longer history with Magomed. He had fought with most of them in both wars with Russia, and trusted all of them with his life. Still, their usefulness had come to an end. For the next phase, he had to move lightly and fast, unencumbered. Too many of his men knew about the stolen bomb, and it didn't take a genius to piece together what Pytor had been doing in the workshop and in the woods with the earthmover.

Pytor was the single exception. The old scientist was exempt from Magomed's cull. With terminal lung cancer, he had a year to live, maybe less. Cutting the original warhead into multiple smaller devices had been more of a personal validation for him than a way to get rich. All he was interested in was collecting his paycheck and spending the rest of his days basking in the glory of his last big mission. Magomed trusted him, but he had placed one condition upon the old man's continued welfare: he had to help Magomed kill the soldiers. He didn't think Pytor would have a problem with that.

"We are almost done, old friend," Magomed said, trying his best to put his thoughts forward to the next phase.

They set off for the garage.

All six men were present when Magomed and Pytor arrived. They leaped to attention as Magomed opened the door.

With a wave of his hand, he instructed them to relax. He took a deep breath. "I've got some good news." He nodded at Pytor, who opened a large plastic cooler sitting on a workbench. He extracted a frosted bottle of Bogorodskaya vodka.

"Thanks to all of you, and especially, thanks to

Pytor," Magomed said with a broad grin, "we have achieved our goal. Our mission is complete."

The men erupted into a round of cheers and whistles. An excited murmur ran through them. Magomed knew they were looking forward to returning to their homes, to their families.

"I would like to celebrate our success," he continued. "Pytor?"

The scientist extracted eight tall shot glasses from the cooler and placed them in a neat line on the edge of his work bench. He unscrewed the cap and poured, filling each glass to the brim, sloshing some on the bench in the process.

"Please," Magomed said, gesturing toward the drinks as soon as Pytor finished.

Each soldier picked up a drink. Magomed and Pytor waited until the soldiers had theirs, and then picked up their own, taking care not to allow their skin to come in contact with any stray moisture on the glasses.

Magomed raised his glass. "To a successful mission! Salut!"

As one, his men downed their drinks in a single shot. All except for the young soldier from the clearing the day before. He hesitated, holding his drink before his lips, sniffing at it.

The effects of the Prussic acid, or hydrogen cyanide-laced vodka, were instantaneous. A single glass crashed to the floor, shattering on the chipped concrete. Then another. All five men who had ingested the poisoned alcohol collapsed to their knees, and then to the floor, writhing and grasping at their throats. Their color quickly changed from ruddy pink to a sickly blue as their bodies lost the ability to process oxygen. They grasped at their throats, their mouths foaming as the poison attacked their cells, shutting down nervous systems and causing hearts to go into violent and terminal fibrillation. The stench of fresh shit exploded in the closed room as the dying men voided their bowels.

"Why...?" The remaining soldier flung his glass away and turned to run.

Magomed hadn't counted on that. Before the young man had made it a meter, Magomed's pistol boomed, and a neat hole appeared in the soldier's back. The soldier stumbled and pitched forward face-down onto the cool concrete. Magomed walked over to him and put a second bullet into the back of the soldier's head.

"I'm sorry," he whispered. Still holding his drink in his left hand, Magomed re-holstered his weapon. He carefully placed his shot glass back on the workbench next to the almost full bottle. The stench was terrible—cordite laced with fresh shit and urine, the odor of a slaughterhouse.

Pytor splashed his drink on the floor. The vodka and cyanide mixture would evaporate quickly, leaving no trace. He went to the closest man and nudged the body with his boot. Then he took out his cigarettes and offered the pack to Magomed.

Magomed accepted one, even though he didn't normally smoke. It would help cover the smell. "That last soldier, the one who ran..."

"I know," Pytor said. "I do not like it when they run."

Magomed shook his head. "Nor do I. It is so undignified."

He crossed the room to the van. Opening the rear door, he gazed at the six plastic cases stacked over the rear axle. Two, the radiological bombs, were marked with a white stripe on the handle. He closed the door and turned back to Pytor. "Let's get this mess cleaned up and get out of here. I'll take care of the bodies if you can do another sweep through the compound to ensure we left nothing behind."

Not that Magomed wanted to deal with the dead bodies. He had to haul six men outside, across the asphalt, and into the woods, then dump their bodies into the pit. Once all six men were in place, he would operate the backhoe to fill it in, entombing them with the equipment used to create the bombs. He considered asking Pytor to help, but the haunted look on the old man's face told him he was well past the point of exhaustion.

Pytor set off for the interior of the building.

Alone again, Magomed took a two-by-three-meter plastic tarpaulin from the workbench, shook it out, and set to work moving the corpses.

TWENTY-FIVE

Fifteen Miles Northeast of Nashville

VIKTOR POUNDED HIS HANDS ON the steering wheel in rhythm with the teeth-jarring bass emanating from the speakers in the back of his Expedition, rapping in perfect unison with Eminem's linguistic gymnastics. He couldn't hear his own voice, but he didn't care. The rapping energized him, filled him with a visceral sense of purpose. Closing in on a lumbering tractor trailer, he flicked his turn signal down and shot into the left lane, cutting off a family in a minivan starting their own pass. He jammed down the accelerator and rocketed past the truck. After he put a few dozen car-lengths between it and himself, he drifted into the right lane. The song ended and a new one began.

Traffic was getting heavier, had been for the past ten miles. Checking the speedometer, Viktor realized he was doing eighty. He took his foot off the gas, turned down the volume, and then pulled his phone from the center console. The screen said seven miles. He was almost there.

For such a smart guy, Viktor thought, Greg sure was sloppy. It had been a mere ten hours since he had broken the window in the side door of Greg's suburban garage, ten hours since he had discovered the forgotten Google Maps printout showing detailed driving directions from Washington to an address in downtown Nashville. That Greg had left the printout behind told Viktor how much of a panic he had been in to leave town. Not that he was surprised; if Viktor were being pursued by someone such as himself, he would also be running for his life. But he would be more careful. Of that, he was sure.

Viktor rubbed his eyes with the back of his hand, trying to grind the sleep away. It was the day that would never end. It seemed he had been on the move his whole life, though in reality, it had only been a little over three days. He was beat. He wanted nothing more than to be done with his mission so his bosses in Moscow would get off his back and let him get back to his regular life, whatever that was now. He grimaced at the thought of his last conversation with Alexander Yolkin, only a few hours before as he was merging onto I-81 South. Yolkin had been furious, demanding an explanation as to why Viktor hadn't returned his two previous calls. In hindsight, Viktor knew he could have played it better, but Yolkin had caught him off guard, and he had said the first thing that came to his mind. Telling Yolkin he was dealing with it, and that he would get back to them when he was good and ready, had not been the wisest choice of words. He suspected he would pay for them at some point. But not today. He had cut Yolkin off and turned off his phone. He didn't need the distraction. He would call back when he was done.

He passed under a broad green and white sign indicating his exit was one mile ahead. He slipped the phone back into the console and moved into the far right lane. The road had gone from two lanes in each direction to four in the last few miles.

Viktor killed the stereo as he rolled down the exit ramp. He sat up a little straighter and focused on his surroundings. According to the directions, Jenny Cooper's apartment building was barely three miles off the interstate. Two quick rights, straight for a mile, and then a left on Woodlawn. Easy as pie.

The speed limit dropped to thirty-five. Viktor slowed further. The last few miles flew by, and before he knew it, he was at his destination. The modest neighborhood appeared like any suburban neighborhood around the country. A mix of medium- and low-density buildings stretched north and south, their sameness punctuated by a periodic strip mall or gas station. Number 146 was a five-story building. All glass on the outside, it practically sparkled in the early morning sunlight.

He got lucky and found a pull-through parking spot. It gave him easy access to the road and good visibility in both directions on the street. From the rear of the truck, Viktor retrieved a black nylon tool bag and a hat that read "Cap's Plumbing." He put on the hat and took a look at himself in the rearview mirror. Viktor thought he looked foolish, but it would work. He hefted the bag, feeling the weight of his gun and two extra magazines of ammunition. From his shirt pocket, he extracted a pair of foam earplugs. He fit one into each ear, and all he could hear was the muffled roar of blood swooshing through his own arteries.

A minute later, he was inside the empty lobby, tracing his finger across the directory. Jenny Cooper—318. He smiled, pleased with himself. It was going to be easier than he thought.

Noting the position of the door to the stairwell in

relation to the front doors, Viktor stepped into a waiting elevator and pressed the button for the third floor. The doors whisked shut, and the elevator lurched to life, traveling at a snail's pace to the third floor. While he waited for the door to open, he unzipped his bag enough to slip his hand inside. He touched the cold metal of the gun and caressed it, reassured.

The door trundled open, revealing a dimly lit hallway decorated with a faded maroon carpet and beige walls. A sign directly in front of him directed him to the right. He followed the arrow. Apartment 318 was located four doors down, on the right. Viktor paused to memorize his bearings. The stairway door was the closest door to the elevator, only two doors back. That was the way he would leave.

He had no idea if anyone was home. Checking his watch, he made a mental note of the time. Pressing the buzzer on the left side of the door, he angled his head down so anyone looking through the peephole wouldn't be able to make out his face. He put his hand in his bag again and wrapped his fingers around the gun grip.

The lock clicked, and the door swung open a few inches. Viktor looked up and smiled, taking care not to make direct eye contact. He needed to maintain the element of surprise.

"Can I help you?" a man asked. Not Greg.

Viktor pulled his gun and charged into the door with his right shoulder, knocking it open and sending the man inside reeling out of sight. Viktor followed close behind, and once inside, he kicked the door shut with his heel and dropped his bag on the floor. He saw movement out of the corner of his eye. A woman, Jenny he supposed, dashed down the hall, away from him.

Viktor aimed at the head of the young man who had answered the door and pulled the trigger. His gun roared, and a bright fan of blood appeared on the wall as the man crumpled to the floor. Through the earplugs, it sounded like distant fireworks on a summer night. He stalked toward the rear of the apartment.

"Greg? We need to talk."

No response. Instead, a door slammed shut somewhere down the hall, and a young woman screamed. Viktor laughed. *Pointless.* He strode down the hall, passing a bathroom on his right and then two empty bedrooms on his left. The last door on the right was closed.

Viktor stopped short. *Could Greg have a gun?* He dismissed the thought immediately. Greg was not the sort of man to carry a firearm, and procuring one on such short notice would have been almost impossible. Stepping forward, Viktor knocked twice on the door with the barrel of his gun.

No reply. He sighed. He had hoped it would be easier. Hoped, but not expected it. Assuming the door was locked, he shot the knob. He knew he could have kicked it in, but he was enjoying himself.

The door swung open.

On the far side of the room, huddled between a queen-sized bed and a dresser, was the girl. Viktor shot her twice, once in the chest and once in the face, and she slumped out of sight. Then, before he could register what was happening, the door slammed into his arm, nearly causing him to drop his weapon.

"You fucker!" Greg screamed.

Viktor didn't hesitate. He squeezed the trigger and shot Greg in the leg. Greg screamed and fell to the floor beside the bed, rolling around in agony.

Viktor went over to him and aimed the gun at his

face. "You really thought I would forget about you? That I wouldn't find you?"

Greg lay there whimpering, trying to staunch the flow of blood from his thigh. He grew paler by the second, but he still refused to meet Viktor's eyes.

With a disgusted shake of his head, Viktor pulled the trigger twice more.

He checked his watch. *Seventy-four seconds from start to finish. Not bad.*

Taking care to stay out of the spreading pool of blood, Viktor collected his shell casings. Next, he collected the casing from the bullet in the other man's body. Once he finished, he retrieved his bag and dropped his handgun and the shell casings into it. He pulled out the blue and white can of Kingsford lighter fluid from the bottom of the bag, and with a quick press of his thumb, he popped open the lid and sent a stream of inflammable piss around the room, making sure to soak every horizontal surface as thoroughly as possible.

Viktor closed the lid on the empty can and stuffed it back into his bag. He paused for a moment to take out his ear plugs. Then, he listened. Somewhere far off in the distance, he thought he heard the sound of sirens. Or maybe not. He shrugged.

Viktor withdrew a plastic Bic lighter, purchased at the same Walmart in Bristol where he had purchased the lighter fluid. He spun the rough metal wheel, and a small flame appeared. He took a step back toward the door, to the end of the line he had traced in the carpet with the lighter fluid. Kneeling, he touched the flame to the soaked carpet. At first it didn't seem to want to catch. He cursed. Then, just as he was about to extinguish the flame and try for a bigger one, the lighter fluid caught fire. Viktor only had a moment to move as the flame raced across the floor to the other side of the room where he had squirted the bulk of the lighter fluid.

Viktor ran.

TWENTY-SIX

Annapolis, Maryland
Later That Afternoon

WITH A RISING SENSE OF excitement, Darlene clicked on the highlighted link and leaned forward to read the new information on the screen. A soft gasp escaped her mouth few moments later.

"No way," she said to her empty office. "How in the world did this woman get access to our systems?"

Her secure phone rang. She picked it up, not paying attention to the caller ID. "Darlene Foster."

"Darlene. It's Kurt."

She heard traffic in the background. "You must still be in D.C.," she said.

"Yeah. I just finished meeting with Dominic. We had quite an interesting discussion."

Darlene perked up. "Really? What did he have to say?"

"Pretty much what we suspected. Helen was telling the truth. They've been working it through diplomatic channels so far, trying to keep it quiet."

Darlene hit *Print* and sent the current page to the printer on the other side of her office. "I knew it. Are you coming back this afternoon?" she asked.

"I am. But I have to take care of a few things here first. I should be back in a few hours."

Darlene clicked to a different window. "Good. I think I may be onto something..."

Kurt coughed. "Really? What is it?" Although he was on a secure phone, the traffic noise made it painfully obvious that he was outside, in a non-secure location.

Darlene spoke louder. "I'm not sure yet, but I think I'm starting to see a pattern forming around Melody Jackson." Kurt was silent for a moment, prompting her to add, "It may be nothing, though; I don't want to get your hopes up.

"I understand. Let me know as soon as you're sure, even if it turns out to be a dead end."

"I will. Don't worry."

"Okay. I'll talk to you in a little while." She hung up and returned her attention to the computer screen, which displayed a graphical representation of Melody Jackson's movements in weeks leading up to the attack. The information came from several sources, including her mobile telephone, her purchasing history from her credit and debit cards, and the records from a network of automated tollbooths in the D.C. metro area. According to the data, Melody had spent most of her time coming and going to work in downtown Washington, with a few side trips outside the District.

Those side trips were what had Darlene excited. Her software had combed through the data and assigned a weighted, color-coded score to each cluster of geo-locations depending on a host of factors she had selected: time, duration, frequency, and the purpose of the visit. Of the variables, the purpose of the visit was the most speculative and, at the same time, the most intriguing.

Three clusters stood out in particular. She clicked on the first. Melody had visited a bar in Georgetown seven times over the course of three weeks. Darlene flipped back to Melody's personnel file and traced her finger down the screen, searching for her behavioral profile. It was near the bottom of the page. According to the report, culled from her military service dossier as well as prior civilian health records, Melody didn't drink. What, then, was she doing at a bar? Darlene scribbled *Drinking problem?* on her notepad. *And why did she return to the same bar over and over again?* She accessed the city records pertaining to the bar and found nothing unusual to note. No health violations. No Alcoholic Beverage Regulation Administration citations. Nothing.

Slightly disappointed, she moved on to the next data set, a cluster of eleven visits to a townhouse complex in Arlington. She instructed the computer to search for correlations. She got an answer a few seconds later. The townhouse belonged to Melody's boyfriend, Josh Carpenter, twenty-eight, a graduate of the University of Virginia and an attorney at a lobbying firm. She moved on.

The next data point intrigued her, not for the number of visits, which was small, but for the lack of obvious correlating factors and the temporal proximity to Melody's final days. The visits spanned a period of three consecutive nights from roughly nine o'clock in the evening until nearly dawn the following morning. The most recent visit had occurred several days before the attack on the SEWS infrastructure. Another boyfriend? Darlene wondered. *No.* It didn't fit her personality. She flipped to Melody's personnel file and read some more. Engaged. Due to be married in the fall, Melody had filed papers with the Marine Corps, notifying them she would be traveling out of the country, to the Bahamas, for her wedding. *Definitely not another boyfriend.*

Darlene felt the familiar tickle of an imminent *Aha* moment skirting the periphery of her consciousness. All she had to do was put it together. She opened up a satellite view of the location and inspected the image. It showed a house in suburban Silver Spring, Maryland. Nothing special. With a few keystrokes, Darlene navigated to the Silver Spring property records database and began to read.

According to the records, the house was owned by a man named Greg Miller. *This has to be it,* she told herself. She took the name and submitted it to the FBI databases for a preliminary background check. That would take a few minutes, she knew from experience. Rather than sit and wait, she decided to take a quick break. Pushing back from her desk, she set off in search of a cold drink and something to munch on.

~ * * * ~

Ten minutes later, Darlene was back at her desk, her fingers flying over her keyboard in an almost inhuman blur. The solution had come to her while she was sipping a Cherry Coke in the break room. If Greg Miller was somehow connected with Melody in the past week, and the FBI didn't already know about it, then there was no reason to believe she would find something they hadn't. The FBI search was still running. She left it alone and opened a new search window, configuring it to scan local news sites and public police department records across the country.

Biting her lip, she hit *Enter.*

Her computer beeped right away, signaling a hit. Curious, Darlene scooted closer to her computer.

Nashville, Tennessee
Deadly Fire Claims Three

Darlene clicked the link and skimmed the text. According to the *Tennessean*, a Nashville news web site, a man named Greg Miller, a woman named Jennifer Cooper, and another man named Paul Sloan had perished in a structure fire the previous evening. Police weren't releasing further details at the present.

"This can't be a coincidence," Darlene mused aloud. "Let's see what's really going on." She navigated to the Nashville Police website, wormed her way through their security and into their internal database, and pulled up the case details. The internal notes were far more damning than the sanitized press release. According to police records, all three victims had died of gunshot wounds *before* the fire was set. The police suspected the fire had been started intentionally to cover the murders, and they were treating the case as a triple homicide. Now *that* was something she could work with.

Darlene took a deep breath and assessed her findings. Greg Miller was definitely connected. How, she wasn't quite sure. Still, she was missing something. With Greg Miller dead and Melody Jackson nowhere to be found, she couldn't help but believe there was yet another person involved, someone cleaning up after himself. The boyfriend was out. That left the bar. There had to be someone there, someone at the center of it all.

Opening another window, she navigated to the D.C. public records database and kicked off a more exhaustive search, looking for detailed ownership records, financial dealings, and anything else that may indicate abnormal activity. The results came back right away. The bar was owned by a man named Viktor Durov, had been for seven years. Her heart caught in her throat when she realized that might be her connection. With shaking hands, Darlene copied his name and pasted it into an NSA search tool that would troll through a variety of national and international databases. She didn't have to wait long, as her screen began to fill with information on Viktor Durov—his criminal background, his arrests, and most important of all, a link to his father's secret FBI dossier. Curious, Darlene followed the link. She examined the senior Durov's dossier and nearly fell out of her chair when she saw that he was a former KGB officer and naturalized citizen of the United States.

In her excitement, it took her two tries to dial Kurt's number correctly.

TWENTY-SEVEN

The White House
At the Same Time

LEANING BACK IN HIS PLUSH leather executive chair, Dominic put his feet on the corner of his desk and fished in his pocket for his nicotine lozenges. He pulled out the slim blue tube, flicked open the lid with his thumb, and shook out one of the cherry-flavored tablets. It had been eight weeks since he had given up smoking at the insistence of his teenage daughter Sophie, and so far, he hadn't fallen off the wagon. The lozenges did the trick, although he still felt an unmistakable tug whenever he passed someone puffing on a cigarette.

He reached for his desk and pulled a yellow legal pad onto his lap. The top sheet of the notebook was covered with scribbles, stick-figure doodles he had made while on the phone with the state department a half-hour earlier. The news was no better than the last time he had checked. The Russians weren't saying anything about the attack on the SEWS computers or about the bomb. He didn't blame them. If the tables were turned, the White House would clam up just as fast. Fortunately, that wasn't the case. Dominic couldn't imagine what he would do if a nuke ever got loose within the borders of the United States. If that were to happen, he hoped it wasn't on his watch. On second thought, he hoped it was. He wouldn't want anyone else to have to deal with that kind of stress. He chuckled at himself. What was it about his job that kept him coming back? He had never thought of himself as exceptional, and that, the President had told him, was one of the reasons he had nominated him for the job in the first place, despite their party differences and a long line of people with far better credentials. *No*, Dominic thought. If a nuke ever gets loose inside this country, I'm sure whoever is sitting in this chair will be capable of handling the situation as well as, or better than, I could.

He flipped to a new page and pulled a pen from his breast pocket. He had an electronic tablet on the other end of his desk, but he still thought better with pen and paper, to the endless consternation of the White House staff, who insisted every scrap of correspondence be digitized for posterity. As much as Dominic would love to shred his doodles and musings, it simply wasn't an option. Someone far in the future would inevitably want to look back through the historical record for meanings in his actions, and who was he to deny that sort of hindsight?

On the left side of the page, he wrote Kurt's name in capital letters. Underneath, he wrote Amanda's and Darlene's names. On the right side, he made an entry for the bomb in Russia and an entry for the hacker attack. Across the bottom, he jotted down the major government agencies that could, and probably should be, involved in resolving both situations: CIA, NSA,

DIA, NRO, and the FBI. To date, he and President Cooper had granted limited operational authority to Kurt and Darlene. Amanda was still a wild-card. He hadn't heard anything in the last twenty-four hours about her situation in Canada, and was beginning to expect the worst. He drew a line through her name. It was safe, he thought, to assume she wouldn't assist in the current investigations. He drew a question mark beside Darlene's name. She seemed capable for her age and looked to be a rising star in her home agency. He would have to keep an eye on her, he decided. A more permanent rotation into the White House wasn't out of the question, although she was doing valuable work in her current job with the NSA. It didn't take great imagination to see her in his chair some day in the not too distant future. He smiled at the idea. With a little seasoning, she would do fine in the role, and he had to admit, she would look good on camera, a lot better than the usual stuffed-shirts that typically held the job.

His thoughts drifted to his conversation with Kurt the day before. Dominic liked Kurt, as a professional and as a man. Kurt had gone through hell and back with the loss of his brother and his family, and he seemed to be holding up well. Kurt reminded him of himself in a distant sort of way. Dominic did wonder how long Kurt would hold up under the pressure cooker of D.C. politics. Keeping him at arms' length from the day-to-day stress was a good strategy for the short term, but he couldn't maintain it forever. At some point, Kurt would re-enter the real world and be forced to play nice with other people. The crisis would end; they always did. When that happened, Kurt would have to make a choice. Either he would drop back into his role as an analyst at the CIA, or he would leave government service for good. Dominic didn't see much middle ground. There was a slight possibility that the President could carve out a place for Kurt on his staff, but he doubted Kurt would be satisfied with that. He didn't think Kurt would be satisfied with returning to the CIA, either. There were too many bad memories there, from his brother to people like Helen Bartholomew and her dead conspirators.

In the margin, he drew a stack of teetering three-dimensional blocks threatening to spill from the edge of the page. And then he had an idea. Maybe... maybe a transfer into the operations directorate would work for Kurt? *That wouldn't be so different from what he was doing right now, would it?* Dominic made a note to himself to get in touch with Paul Pungley, the director of the CIA, to see if there was a role for Kurt, something that would allow him to grow and use his newfound skills and contacts. Director Pungley, of course, had been living on borrowed time since the stolen bomb fiasco, so Dominic would have to move fast. Congress was already calling for Pungley's head, suggesting a new director was the only way to save the tarnished credibility of the CIA. After a call with the director the previous evening, he had come away with the distinct impression he was speaking to a dead man.

Dominic's phone rang. He dropped his feet from his desk and scooted forward to answer it.

"Mr. Velasquesz," the head of the President's Secret Service detail said. "There's been an incident. President Cooper... he's dead."

Dominic dropped the phone and leaped to his feet, sending his chair spinning out of control as he raced for the Oval Office.

TWENTY-EIGHT

Makhachkala, Dagestan

AT THE ENTRANCE TO THE high-walled compound, the silver Mercedes sedan slowed to a crawl long enough for the three-meter-tall reinforced iron gate to rumble to the side. With a throaty roar, the car surged through the gap, and the gate slid shut behind it.

The driver brought the car to an abrupt stop, and Magomed grabbed the suitcase on the seat next to him as it threatened to tumble to the floor. "Fool!" he yelled at the driver in Russian. "You must be more careful!"

The driver mumbled an apology, but before Magomed could berate him further, he was out of the car and circling around to the rear door. He yanked it open and stepped to the side, giving his employer a wide berth.

Magomed slid from the vehicle, dragging the heavy suitcase behind him across the supple leather seats. He secretly hoped it left a mark. As he got to his feet, he gave the driver a withering glare, but held his tongue. It wasn't the time to appear out of control. He had a deal to consummate, and as in any business transaction, a confident appearance was half of the battle.

The compound was larger on the inside than it appeared from the street. Taking up an entire city block, it housed four separate buildings, including a main office complex, a five-vehicle garage, a small barracks for the ever-present guard staff, and an additional, smaller building, which was Magomed's destination. It had been over two years since he had visited the compound and its owner, two years in which he had redefined his place in the world.

A pair of guards flanked the front door of the smaller structure. Each wore a dour expression and cradled an assault rifle. As Magomed approached, the guard on the right raised a small handheld radio to his lips and uttered a few words. He listened for a response and then clipped the radio back to his belt.

"Good afternoon, Mr. Gasanov," the guard addressed him in Russian. "He is waiting for you."

"Spasibo," Magomed said. The guard opened the door and ushered Magomed inside.

The main chamber of the building belied the bland construction of the exterior. All polished chrome and blond wood, it reminded Magomed of the inside of a Danish furniture store, complete with a swooping ultra-modern white leather couch and a clear acrylic coffee table atop a tufted carpet that, to his amusement, looked like a sea of waving pastel-blue pasta. He had never understood his old friend's taste in decor, and had long ago given up trying to reconcile the dichotomy between battle-hardened soldier and connoisseur of all things Danish.

"Magomed!" a disembodied voice cried from the far side of the room. "Welcome back!"

Magomed forced a smile and lowered his suitcase

to the floor. He set off across the field of limp pasta in the direction of the familiar voice. As he approached the middle of the room, a giant of a man stepped from behind a dense cluster of ficus trees. The man held a small spray bottle in one hand and a rag in the other.

Standing at least a foot taller than Magomed and outweighing him by a hundred pounds, give-or-take, Maksud Alam embodied the rough and tumble former-warrior stereotype down to the jagged pink scar arcing across his left cheekbone. He exuded an animal power, a sense of bottled rage primed to explode any moment, which made Magomed look like a timid schoolteacher in contrast. Still, the men had become fast allies during the first Chechen conflict, and their partnership had continued over the years, with them frequently trading behind-the-scenes support in their respective bids for independence.

Maksud approached Magomed, his arms held wide. They kissed on the cheek, the thick whiskers of Maksud's unshaven face tickling Magomed's lips. They each took a step back, observing the other. It had been a long time since they had spoken in person.

"Come, come," Maksud said in English, gesturing toward the low-slung leather couch. "I see you brought something for me." His eyes glinted with excitement.

"I did," Magomed said. "As promised." Retrieving the suitcase, Magomed made his way to the couch. He placed the suitcase in the center of the Lexan table, closer to Maksud than himself.

"That is it?" Maksud asked. "It is so small."

Magomed allowed himself a smile at the compliment. "Yes. My engineer was very creative."

Maksud edged closer to the device. "May I see?"

"Of course." With both thumbs, Magomed popped the two latches on the front. Stealing a glance at Maksud, he saw the man holding his breath, about to burst from anticipation. He lifted the lid, exposing the dark interior. "The yield is roughly twenty kilotons." He pointed at the plastic numeric keypad. Fishing inside the foam on the lid of the case, he extracted a printed piece of paper. "Instructions. In both English and Russian."

Maksud reached toward the keypad, but Magomed pushed his hand aside. "Careful! There are no safety controls. You set the timer and get as far away as possible before it detonates."

Maksud tentatively placed his hand on the hard plastic bump in the center of the device. He glanced at Magomed with a devious smile. "It's warm."

"Yes. That is the core."

Maksud yanked his hand back as if he had touched a burning stove top. "Is it safe?"

"As safe as it can be. It is shielded, of course. But I would not place my balls on it unless I wanted a kid with three arms and six legs."

Maksud nodded. "I think I've seen enough."

"Are you sure?"

Maksud scooted back on the couch, putting some distance between him and the weapon. "Yes. I am sure."

"Okay." Magomed closed the case and sat back. He pulled out a pack of cigarettes and offered one to Maksud. Maksud waved him off, and Magomed proceeded to light his own. "So..."

"Hold that thought. I'll be right back." Maksud hoisted his bulk from the couch and ducked through an undersized door next to the ficus trees.

Magomed heard hurried whispering from the other side. He forced himself to stay calm, well aware that if the Dagestani decided to rip him off, it would happen soon.

Maksud re-entered the room a minute later,

carrying a suitcase almost identical to the version Magomed had brought. Moving Magomed's suitcase from the table, he placed his own in its place and opened it.

Inside the case were bundles of neatly stacked euros and U.S. dollars, tightly wrapped in stretch plastic, filling every square inch of available space. "This is the cash you requested. The balance has been wired to your account as instructed."

Magomed sifted through the money, doing a quick mental tally. It contained four hundred thousand in each currency, in a mix of bill sizes, enough money to tide him over until he was able to launder and process the remaining balance in his Swiss account. He pulled out his phone and logged into his bank, smiling as he confirmed the presence of the balance.

"I think we are done then," Magomed announced. "As always, it has been a pleasure doing business with you. It has been far too long."

Maksud put a hand on Magomed's shoulder. "Why the hurry, old friend? Have a drink before you go. I insist."

Magomed ran a quick mental calculation. The hidden timer embedded in the bottom of the bomb was set for five hours. That left just enough time for him to return to the airport and get most of the way across Europe before Maksud and his ridiculous Danish furniture collection were reduced to atoms.

"I'm sorry," he said with a calculated frown. "But I have to catch a flight. Next time. I promise."

A flash of annoyance crossed Maksud's face, replaced in an instant with the stony acceptance of a man accustomed to operating on a tight schedule. "Of course. I understand."

Magomed got to his feet and extended his hand. "Until next time." Collecting his suitcase, Magomed set off for the door, a new spring in his step.

~ * * * ~

The Mercedes bumped onto the main street outside the compound, the heavy-duty suspension soaking up the irregularities of the pitted street as if they didn't exist. Expending a bomb to kill Maksud was not the most efficient use of his limited resources, Magomed knew, but it would solve two very real and persistent problems. First, it would eliminate a competitor in the region, one who, while seeming to offer unconditional assistance, had recently shown strong indications of being under control of the Russians. Second, and more important, it would send an unmistakable signal to Moscow that Magomed meant business.

"Wake me when we get to the airport," he told the driver as he closed his eyes.

"Of course, sir."

TWENTY-NINE

Georgetown
M Street

KURT PULLED OUT HIS PHONE and navigated to the front page of the CNN website. President Cooper's death dominated the headlines. The aortal aneurysm had killed him instantly, Dominic had told him the previous day. Kurt had offered his deepest condolences, and while Dominic had said the right words in return, Kurt could tell he was beyond devastated. Dominic and President Cooper's relationship went all the way back to Yale, and despite their political differences, they had played on each other's strengths, forging a coherent national security policy that set a new standard.

"I still can't believe it," Kurt said, shaking his head. "I mean... he was so full of life... so vibrant..."

Darlene stopped typing and glanced up from her laptop computer. She gave him a tight smile. "I know. He was a good man. To go like that... how's Dominic taking it?"

Kurt shrugged. “He’s pretty broken up, but I think he’ll get through it. I hated to do it, but I asked him what would happen to us, to this operation.”

“Really? What did he say?”

“Not much, only that we’ll have to wait and see. He said everything is in flux, but there shouldn’t be any immediate impact.”

The radio in the front of the van crackled. “We’re a go in two. I repeat. Go in two.”

Kurt tensed involuntarily. Two minutes. Two short minutes until the FBI descended upon Viktor Durov and took him into custody. He wondered if Durov had any idea what was about to land on his head. Probably not, he decided. From what Kurt could see from his position in the surveillance van, the FBI had done an excellent job of infiltrating the neighborhood, to the point where he couldn’t tell who was FBI and who wasn’t unless someone told him.

Durov’s bar, a small but opulent establishment on the busy thoroughfare of M Street in central Georgetown, had been under constant electronic and physical surveillance for the past eight hours, ever since the Foreign Intelligence Surveillance Court had granted them an emergency warrant. Darlene’s analysis indicated with an eighty-nine percent certainty that Durov was the nexus of the attack on the Strategic Early Warning System. According to Special Agent Jacobsen, the head of the FBI team conducting the raid, Greg Miller’s residence was being searched at the same moment. That operation, of course, didn’t have the same level of urgency, considering that Greg Miller was dead.

Kurt locked his phone and tucked it into his pocket.

Darlene snapped her laptop closed and stowed it on an overhead shelf. “No radio traffic in or out in the last ten minutes," she announced with a flash of satisfaction. She had been monitoring Durov's mobile phone traffic, searching for any indication he was aware of the impending raid. She wasn't the only one, of course. At least two more vans full of FBI technicians were stationed nearby, scouring the airwaves for every stray signal flitting through the muggy afternoon air.

"This'll be over fast," she said, almost to herself.

Kurt perked up. "Have you done this before? A raid?" He couldn't help but admire her apparent calm. He was a bundle of nerves, unable to focus on one thing for more than a few seconds at a time. He wanted the raid to be over as fast as possible so they could get on to the business of interrogating Durov to find out how he had orchestrated the attack, and most importantly, if he had anything to do with the bomb in Moscow.

Darlene shook her head. "Nothing this close. I do most of my work behind a keyboard." She smiled, and for the first time, Kurt saw a trace of nervous uncertainty in her face.

Kurt peered out the window, momentarily distracted by a woman pushing a stroller past the entrance to the bar.

The same voice from earlier came on the radio. "We're a go. I repeat. We're a go."

Kurt watched in awe as the person he thought was a mother out for an afternoon walk reached into her stroller and withdrew a wicked-looking tactical shotgun, then turned and charged the front door of the bar. At least a dozen additional agents, all dressed as civilians, materialized from the passing crowd and joined her. As it was midday, the bar should be open, the door unlocked. If for some reason, that wasn't the case, Jacobsen had said that they would enter the establishment by breaking down the glass door or ramming through the large plate glass windows flanking it.

"Here we go," Kurt whispered. He pressed his face against the window of the van and held his breath.

There was a muffled pop, and Kurt jumped. He wasn't sure, but it sounded like it came from behind him. "Was that a shot?"

Darlene didn't answer right away. She scanned the street. "I think it was a car backfiring."

Kurt let out his held breath. Taking Durov alive was crucial. If he died during the raid, their investigation would end right here in the back of the van. Darlene had been working overtime on the NSA computer systems, digging deep into the recesses of Durov's past, searching for some connection, an unusual financial transaction or any anomaly that would provide the link between Durov and whoever was running things behind the scenes. So far, it had been a series of dead ends, threads of interest that invariably ran out before leading to anything useful. What they did know was that Durov had been born to a Russian father who coincidentally happened to have been a KGB officer under the Soviet regime. Still, there was no guarantee that the Russians were behind the attack. It had been a long time since Viktor's father had died, and as Viktor was himself a mid-level Mafia member, there were almost infinite possibilities as to who could have been pulled the strings. Still, the Russians were the most likely suspects at the moment.

A burly middle-aged man stepped from the entrance and looked in their direction. He spoke into a handheld radio. "We got your man."

Kurt let out a whoop. "Yes!" He hauled open the heavy van door and leaped out. After turning to ensure

Darlene was following, he dashed across the street. He arrived at the front door as a swarm of FBI and Capitol police vehicles screeched to a stop behind him. Holding up his ID, he threaded through the agents clustered at the door. "Kurt Vetter and Darlene Foster. We need to see the suspect right away."

The FBI agents made room for them to pass, and Kurt pushed into the bar with Darlene in tow.

The first thing he noticed was the number of people crowded into the small space. The bar was very upscale, well-appointed in rich wood and dark leather with a polished wood floor. A half-dozen small tables were clustered near the front door, and a row of booths with plush maroon leather cushions lined the far wall. All of the action was occurring at the rear of the room. A cluster of agents formed a semicircle around a man pressed face-first against the wall.

Kurt slipped through the semicircle, drawing glares from a few of the FBI agents who had just risked their lives to apprehend Durov.

"Is this him?" Kurt asked, turning toward Agent Jacobsen, a steely man in his mid-forties with collar-length brown hair and dressed in a Washington Bullets T-shirt, tan cargo shorts, and flip-flops.

Jacobsen was dialing his phone. "It is. We just gave him his rights. He's not talking." As he put his phone to his ear, Jacobsen twirled his finger in the air and said, "Turn him around."

One of the other FBI agents spun Durov so he faced Kurt and Darlene.

"That's definitely him," Darlene said from over Kurt's shoulder.

Kurt did a double-take. Durov was dressed in tan slacks, a powder-blue Oxford shirt, and polished brown leather shoes. The only thing that hinted at his true identity was the coldness in his eyes, a look that could have frozen him in place.

"Viktor Durov," Kurt said.

Durov remained expressionless.

"Was there anyone else here?" Kurt asked Jacobsen.

Still talking on the phone, the agent gestured over Kurt's shoulder.

Kurt turned his head and saw a small group of men and women huddled near the front door. He mentally chided himself for missing them on the way in. "Who are they?"

"Patrons, we think," Jacobsen answered as he closed his phone. "We'll talk to all of them, but I think they were just in the wrong place at the wrong time."

Kurt's mind raced. "What about the kitchen staff?"

"They're in custody. We'll question them, too."

Kurt didn't know what else to say. Durov was in custody with no shots fired. That was the last thing he had expected. "Let's get him downtown. I want to get started as soon as possible."

With a final glance at Durov, Kurt turned and strode from the bar.

THIRTY

The White House

DOMINIC BROKE HIS EMBRACE WITH former First Lady Anne Cooper and took a step back. Using his thumb and forefinger, he pinched away the tears that had sprung up in the corners of his eyes. He tried to paste some semblance of a smile on his face.

By all accounts, the former First Lady appeared to be holding up far better than he had expected. Of course, as the former First Lady, she had the luxury of privacy in which to grieve; Dominic still had a job to do. Although the hacker had been apprehended, the Russian warhead was still out there somewhere, and he couldn't rest until he knew where.

Anne put her hand on his shoulder. "I'd like for you to speak at his funeral."

Fresh tears came to Dominic's eyes. Speeches at presidential funerals were typically reserved for important politicians and dignitaries, not lowly political appointees. He knew she meant well, but he also knew there was no way in hell he would get a word in during the ceremony. Still, he didn't want to say anything to bring her down. "I'd be honored."

Anne lowered herself into a soft leather wingback chair, one of the former President's favorites. She smoothed her skirt and stared out the window. "I feel so lost without him..."

Dominic wasn't sure how to respond. He felt the same way, but he needed to show strength, to demonstrate he had everything under control. He had to find a way to put his grief in a box on a shelf far back in his mind until some point in the future, when he had time to let himself fall apart. Over the course of a lifetime, he and President Cooper had forged a well-oiled working relationship. The idea of starting over fresh with a new boss depressed him, so much so that he was entertaining thoughts of leaving government service entirely, retiring and spending more time with his family. Not that he would ever admit that to Anne.

He pulled his nicotine lozenges from his pocket and slid one into his mouth. It didn't satisfy his craving for a smoke, not by a mile.

"What's that?" Anne asked.

"Nicotine."

"That's right. Paul told me you were trying to quit. Good for you."

Dominic cracked a grin. "We'll see how long I last. Right now, a cigarette sounds like the best thing in the world, you know?"

Anne gave him a meek smile. "I know. Believe me."

"How is the planning going?" Dominic asked, knowing full well Anne wouldn't have a clue, but stretching for something to talk about.

Anne gave him a noncommittal shrug. "Full speed ahead, according to the Secret Service."

"That's good." Dominic had run out of things to say. He wanted nothing more than to get away, to return to his office, maybe even head out to Annapolis and meet with Kurt, anything to take his mind off of Rick's death. "I... um, should be going now," he mumbled. "I've got a lot of work to do."

Anne was staring out the window, lost in the bright summer afternoon. "I understand. Thank you for stopping by." She stood, indicating the meeting was over.

"It's my pleasure," Dominic said. "Please call me if you need to talk. I mean it." He took a step toward the door.

Anne held up a finger. "There's one more thing you need to know."

Dominic cocked his head. "Yes?"

"Be careful."

"What do you mean?"

"Nathan," Anne said, referring to former Vice President Nathan Roswell, "has a *unique* perspective on the world. He and Rick didn't always see eye to eye..."

Dominic stared into her eyes, trying to judge the gravity of her words. The fear he saw shook him to his core. "Thank you," he said. "I'll keep that in mind." He wanted to probe, to ask for details, but she was already guiding him to the door.

He had suspected his new boss would be a challenge, that he would have his own agenda. Anne's warning had only confirmed his reservations, as if he didn't already have enough to worry about.

THIRTY-ONE

The White House
Two Days Later

"THANKS FOR STAYING BEHIND," THE former Vice President said. He gestured at one of the couches in the center of the Oval Office. "Please, take a seat."

Dominic complied, pinching up the fabric on his slacks as he dropped onto the couch across from his new boss. He kept his hands in his lap, folded so the President wouldn't see how nervous he was.

President Nathan Roswell had been on the job for a mere forty-eight hours, and, he was already making moves to reshuffle the established order of Washington to fit his own vision. Roswell couldn't have been any different from President Cooper if he had tried. A former senator from Nevada, he had been brought onto the presidential ticket as an olive branch to the ultra-conservative wing of the Republican Party. He was the stick while President Cooper had been the carrot, the moderate telegenic everyman. Now that

Roswell was in charge, never mind the fact that he was unelectable on his own, he was intent on putting his own stamp on the remains of the Cooper administration, and he wasn't wasting any time.

Try as he might, Dominic couldn't help but resent the man. Rick Cooper, after all, had been his friend and confidant for as long as he could remember. He had plucked Dominic from a non-political job with the Department of Homeland Security and elevated him to National Security Adviser at a point when Dominic felt there were few, if any, challenges left in his professional life. And now, he was gone.

The funeral was still a few days out, but the business of government didn't stop while the nation mourned, and that meant Dominic had to stay focused.

President Roswell cleared his throat and crossed his legs. He picked up a stack of documents from the end table beside him and read for a moment. Dominic waited, dreading what was coming next.

"So..." the President said, drawing the word out in the flat, monosyllabic way that made Dominic's skin crawl. "Let's talk national security."

Dominic sat up a little straighter. That he could handle. He had been afraid the President was going to launch straight into a diatribe about the way his old friend had run the White House, a speech that he wasn't sure he could have stomached, not with Rick's death so fresh.

"Yes, sir," he said. "What would you like to know?"

President Roswell gave him a blank stare. "Don't you have a briefing prepared?"

Dominic bit back his surprise. "No, sir. Nothing beyond the summary I delivered in the cabinet meeting." Not twenty minutes earlier, he had delivered his standard daily national security briefing, the same briefing he had delivered for the past two years. He had nothing else in his back pocket.

President Roswell placed his papers on the couch, squaring the edges with his fingers so they lay in a neat pile. “Ah, yes. That... That was... fine. But I want your real briefing, the one with the meat. I want the back story.

The back story? Dominic was puzzled. “Sir?”

President Roswell gave an exasperated sigh. “I want the details. I want to know what you think about the situation. The report you delivered earlier... well, it didn’t have any depth. I need to know everything.”

Dominic cringed inside. On one hand, he could see the President’s point. The briefing was dry and formal. He had led off with the arrest of Viktor Durov, and then summarized the other major security issues facing the nation, of which there were few at the moment. He had neglected to bring up his suspicions about the Russians and the missing bomb, instead downplaying his concerns on the third page of his PowerPoint presentation, under miscellaneous security issues. Cabinet meetings were painful to begin with, and unless there was an ongoing crisis, he had learned early on how to stage his information, holding back issues until the supporting background data was available. Typically, he and Rick would talk off the record, with informal discussions in which Dominic gave his old friend his personal insights on which issues he believed were up and coming, which ones were worth watching out for. Maybe that was what President Roswell wanted. Maybe he wanted the same type of back-channel discussion.

“Okay.” Dominic took a minute to describe to President Roswell how the flow of information had worked between himself and President Cooper. He made sure to caveat his explanation by underscoring his longstanding relationship with the former president, and emphasizing that everything discussed had been off the record.

President Roswell considered Dominic's statement for a few seconds before responding. "Look, Dominic. I like you. President Cooper liked you. I've asked around, and everyone I've spoken to agrees you're the best man for the job. But I need someone who will be candid with me all of the time, not hold anything back. I need facts, and I don't have time to draw them out of you. I need you to bring them to me and to let me decide which are important and which I can ignore. Do you understand?"

Dominic nodded. He understood perfectly. The new President, his boss, wanted him to act as a mere conduit, to abdicate his professional responsibility to analyze and summarize the vast quantities of information flowing into the executive branch. "I'll do my best, sir," he said with a thin smile.

The President gave him a stern glare. "That's more like it. Now tell me more about this Russian thing," he said, flipping to the third page.

Dominic was surprised the President had picked up on that. The intelligence was too raw at the moment for anything beyond rank speculation. Not until Kurt and Darlene had more time to analyze it would he be ready to state how much was truth and how much was conjecture.

Still, he had his orders. There wasn't much he could do to avoid the discussion, so he complied. It only took a few minutes to describe the current state of events surrounding the missing bomb. Starting with the deception in the CIA, Dominic walked President Roswell through the timeline leading up to the discovery of the bomb in Moscow. He briefed him on the team that then President Cooper had set up with

Kurt at the head, and Amanda, still incarcerated in Canada, as second in command, and how, with the SEWS hacker under custody, they were shifting their focus to Helen's warnings about the missing bomb.

The President stopped him there. "Wait. You're telling me you're basing this entire investigation on the word of a traitor?"

That caught Dominic off guard. He hadn't considered Helen in those terms. Sure, technically she *was* a traitor, a traitor of the highest order in fact, but she didn't view herself as such. She felt she had been swept up in something larger than herself, that she had been acting in what she thought were the best interests of the country. "Yes, sir."

The President raised his eyebrows in mock surprise. "You're joking, aren't you?"

"No, sir. This is how it works sometimes. You don't get to pick and choose your sources. Prior to the incident in Moscow, Helen Bartholomew had an exemplary record at the CIA. She's in custody now. Her information is credible, if not corroborated."

The President shook his head. "Have you considered at all that she may be misleading you? Playing with you?"

Dominic seethed. He could almost read the President's mind. He knew, in his gut, where their conversation was heading.

"Do you have *any* hard evidence to support Ms. Bartholomew's assertions?" the President asked.

Dominic crossed his legs and ran his sweaty palms along the fabric of his slacks. "Not at the moment, sir, but I have a top-notch NSA asset on the case. She's the one, by the way, who found the hacker. She'll find something."

The President rose and went over to sit behind his desk. "Look. I want this to go away. It's a Russian issue. Not our problem. The more we stick our nose into it, the greater chance it will blow up in our faces and *become* our problem. The country has enough challenges at the moment with the change of power. We need calm and stability. I want you to bury this Russian thing, let it die."

Dominic was dumbfounded. *Let it die? Is he joking?*

He decided to try a different tack "Sir, as your National Security Advisor, I would not recommend that course of action," he said with as much formality as he could muster. "Our source, while suspect, is valid, and if I may add, far more credible than many we have used in the past."

President Roswell smiled, a patronizing, teeth-baring expression that Dominic recalled from the Vice-Presidential debates on television two years before. It was the look of a man about to eat his opponent for lunch. "Your objections are noted. However, my order stands. Bury it."

Dominic was overcome with a sudden urge to storm out of the Oval Office. So strong was the impulse that he had to press down on his knees with his palms to prevent his legs from carrying him away. *This is only temporary*, he told himself. *Once I have more information, I'll be able to convince him this is a real threat.* "Yes, sir. Consider it buried."

The President leaned back in his chair, exhaling as if an enormous weight had been lifted from his shoulders. "Good. I'm glad that's settled." He picked up a stack of papers and made a show of flipping through them. "That will be all."

Dominic was still reeling from the sudden shift in priorities, and it took a moment for him to realize he had been dismissed. He got to his feet, trembling in anger. "Good day, Mr. President." He turned for the door.

"Oh, one more thing," the President said. "I want that special team disbanded. Right away. That's not how I intend to run things here."

Dominic stopped in his tracks. "Disbanded?"

"Yes. Disbanded. Send everyone back to their home agencies. We need to focus on fixing what's broken, rather than creating new bureaucracy."

"But, sir, without this group, we wouldn't have caught the hacker so quickly. They've demonstrated excellent agility in the face of tight deadlines, an ability to bypass normal channels and get things—"

The President's cut him off with a raised hand. "I understand your opinion. However, it is only your opinion. My order stands. Send them home."

Dominic was dumbfounded. His mouth opened and closed, but no words came out. He swallowed hard. "You're making a big mistake, sir."

The President got up and came around his desk to where Dominic stood. "What was that?"

Dominic stared the President in the eye. In the few moments it had taken for the President to cross the room, Dominic had realized his tactical error. It was not the moment to fight. His best strategy was to play along, to let the President believe he was following orders, to initiate the shutdown, but to roll it as slowly as possible. That would only work for so long, though. If they couldn't find the bomber, and fast, it would be over for him in a heartbeat.

"Nothing, sir. I'll take care of it."

The President stared at him, his teeth showing again. A long moment dragged by before he responded. "That's what I wanted to hear. We'll speak soon."

With nothing left to say, Dominic turned and exited the Oval Office, his thoughts churning as he plotted his next steps.

THIRTY-TWO

Washington, DC
FBI Headquarters

DARLENE SHIFTED ON THE HARD wooden bench, searching in vain for a more comfortable position. Cursing under her breath, she heaved herself to her feet and began pacing the hallway.

Kurt glanced up from his phone. "That's not going to make it happen any sooner."

Darlene stopped directly in front of him, put her hands on her hips, and gave him an angry glare. "I know. I just can't stand this waiting. I should be back in Annapolis, online, searching for the bomb." She spun around and resumed pacing.

Kurt sighed and made his own adjustments to his seating position. Fortunately, the bench didn't bother him as much. The waiting was also driving him crazy, though. They had driven into D.C. a few hours earlier to assist in Viktor Durov's interrogation. After the raid in Georgetown, the FBI had brought the suspected hacker to FBI headquarters on Pennsylvania Avenue, where he would be detained until his arraignment the following day. Knowing Durov's connections in the criminal underworld, the government wasn't taking any chances of his fleeing the country.

Not finding any new messages, Kurt gave up and tucked his phone into his pocket. He expected and hoped Dominic would call rather than send him an email or a text about Amanda, but he wasn't leaving anything to chance. Try as he might, losing himself in his work wasn't doing the trick. Between all of the dashing back and forth between D.C. and Annapolis, dealing with Viktor Durov's capture and the immediate fallout, and the potential of yet another loose nuke, his mind was so scattered that Amanda's plight was the only constant. He had tried not to worry, to convince himself too many powerful people knew of her plight for her to be swept under the rug and forgotten. But that only worked for so long. Then, the doubts began to creep in, making him wonder if he was only deluding himself. Would President Roswell continue the effort to have her released? Kurt didn't know. Hell, he didn't even know if the President was involved. From what he could tell from Dominic, the President didn't even know of Amanda's existence.

Kurt jumped as his phone began buzzing in his pocket. The screen showed Dominic's name. His hopes soared.

"Who is it?" Darlene asked, not breaking her stride.

Kurt put the phone to his ear and it emitted two soft beeps, letting him know he had a secure connection. "It's Dominic," he whispered.

Darlene stopped pacing and returned to her seat beside him.

"Dominic?" Kurt said.

"I'm glad I got you. Are you in D.C.?"

"We are."

"Have they started yet?"

Kurt scowled. "No. We're still waiting."

A long pause. "Look, I just got out of a meeting with President Roswell..."

Kurt's stomach clenched at Dominic's tone. "And?"

"Well, I've got some bad news and some really bad news. Which do you want first?"

"Is it about Amanda?"

"No. Worse."

What the hell could be worse? "Let's start with the really bad news then."

Dominic sucked in his breath. "Are you sure?"

"Bad news," Kurt mouthed to Darlene. She raised an eyebrow and leaned in closer.

"Let's hear it," Kurt said into the phone.

"The President has ordered me to disband your organization, effective immediately. He said, and I quote, 'That's not how I intend to run things here,' whatever the hell that means."

Kurt took a moment to process the words. It was the last thing he had expected. A change in leadership, new people, maybe even their absorption into an existing agency, all of those options had crossed his mind. But disbanding them? When they were so close and after so much success? That made no sense.

"Why?" Kurt asked.

"Beats the shit out of me. He's a different man. Different priorities. Take your pick. My guess is he doesn't like your team because it wasn't his idea."

Kurt rolled his eyes. "But we caught Durov. Doesn't that count for anything?"

"It does. Don't panic. I'm going to work on him. Cutting you loose is a stupid idea. I told him so myself."

"You told him it was stupid?" Kurt asked,

incredulous. He couldn't imagine speaking to the President like that, or any boss for that matter.

"Well, not in those exact words," Dominic said with a nervous laugh, "but yes."

A sickening thought flashed into his mind. "What about Amanda?"

"She didn't come up."

Kurt increased his grip on the phone until he thought he might crush it in his hand. Exhaling slowly, he forced himself to calm down. "What do you mean she didn't come up? How in the hell are we going to get her back if my team is being disbanded? Out of sight, out of mind. The President will forget about her like the last election."

Kurt heard the clatter of fingers on a keyboard in the background.

"Sorry about that," Dominic said a few seconds later. "I had to respond to something. Regarding Amanda, don't worry. I'm on top of it. We're close."

As much as Kurt wanted to believe him, he understood the reality and the challenges Dominic faced. The new President was playing musical chairs with his staff and their priorities. Where everything ended up was anyone's guess. For all Kurt knew, Dominic himself could be out of a job at any moment, and where would *that* leave the effort to bring Amanda home? He thought about pressing the point, but decided against it. He was sure Dominic was well aware of the potential pitfalls to the new President's reorganization. "So, you said there was some normal bad news as well?"

Darlene tapped him on the shoulder and pointed down the hall. "I'll be back in a minute." Kurt gave her a weak nod, and she set off at a brisk pace toward the restrooms.

Dominic continued. "The Russian bomb. He wants

us to back off that as well. He thinks it's their problem, something they can deal with without our help. He believes Helen has an axe to grind, that she's feeding us misinformation about outside involvement."

Kurt was speechless. He let the phone fall away from his ear and barely heard the rest of Dominic's words. He closed his eyes and tried to focus, to distance himself mentally from the wave of catastrophe threatening to knock him from the fragile platform of normalcy he had built atop the wreckage of his life.

"Kurt?"

Kurt put the phone back up to his ear. "Sorry."

"I thought I had lost you," Dominic said. "I'm sorry to be the bearer of such bad news. I'm still processing it myself."

Kurt ran his fingers through his hair. "I just don't know what to say. I'm... I don't know..."

"Look. I know this is unexpected. For the short term, I need to ask you to terminate your investigation. Both of you. Take the day off. Take a few days. Go home. Let me work things on my end, and I'll get back to you as soon as I can."

"Sure," Kurt mumbled, not quite believing the words. "I'll do that."

"Hey!" Dominic said, a new sense of urgency in his voice. "Don't worry. We'll get things fixed. Just be patient."

"I'll talk to you soon," Kurt said.

"Very soon, I hope," Dominic said, his voice rising with forced enthusiasm before he terminated the call.

Kurt lingered, staring at the phone as if were some venomous insect, unable to disengage his mind from the disastrous conversation. His day, his life, had once again come to a screeching halt, and he had no idea what to do next. He dropped the phone into his pocket and turned in the direction Darlene had gone, searching for her face among the crowd of people milling at the end of the hallway. He spotted her steadily working her way in his direction. She was on the phone, her mouth turned down in a deep frown.

Like a man heading to his execution, Kurt set off to intercept her.

THIRTY-THREE

The White House

DOMINIC'S TABLET BEEPED WITH A ten-minute warning for a conference call with the Secretary of Defense. Turning to his computer, he opened a document describing troop levels in Afghanistan, the subject of the meeting, and began to read. His office phone rang before he was able to complete the first sentence.

He took the call from his assistant with a sigh. "What is it, Mary?"

"I have Mr. Maxwell Riggs of the Canadian Security Intelligence Service on the line, sir."

Dominic's breath caught in his throat. He hadn't expected such a quick response. "Put him through. And please push my meeting with SecDef by an hour. If you can't move it, then reschedule for tomorrow."

"Yes, sir," Mary said.

The line clicked once, and he was connected.

"Mr. Riggs," Dominic said. "I hope you're calling with good news."

Riggs cleared his throat. "I am. I want to let you

know Ms. Carter is en route to Washington as we speak. She's on a Holloway charter into Reagan."

Dominic broke into an enormous grin at the news. He leaned his chair back and put his feet on the edge of his desk. "Well, that's about the best news I've heard all day. On behalf of the United States government, I'd like to thank you for seeing our position."

"Believe me, Mr. Velasquez, this decision was not made lightly. In the end, the continuing cooperation between our countries, along with Ms. Carter's recent actions in Moscow and their implications on *our* national security, made the decision to release her the most appropriate. Understand, however, the charges for which we brought her back to stand trial still stand. Ms. Carter is—or at least has been—a loose cannon, and I advise you to keep a careful eye on her."

Dominic considered the warning for a long moment before dismissing it. Everyone had a past, and in Amanda's line of business, the past could somctimes be reprehensible. He would keep an eye on her, but he would give her the benefit of the doubt. "I understand. Thank you. I—"

"One more thing," Riggs interjected. "Ms. Carter is never to step foot on Canadian soil again. If we receive so much as a hint that she is in our territory, this deal is terminated. Do you understand?"

Dominic dropped his feet and sat up straight. "I understand. And I appreciate your candor on the situation."

"Okay, then. Good luck with Ms. Carter. You're going to need it."

The call ended. Dominic placed the phone back in the cradle and switched to his outside line. He dialed Kurt.

"We've got her," he said.

THIRTY-FOUR

Leninkent, Dagestan
18:56:05 MSK (Moscow Standard Time)

MOHAMMED NOTICED A SUBTLE SHIFT in the road noise coming from the tires of the burly GAZ-2330 Tiger. They were slowing. Up ahead, less than a kilometer away, was a gas station, a decrepit, ancient building with three rusty pumps out front and two small, dirty windows facing the road.

"Maksud said no stopping," he reminded his brother Nasir. "He said to go straight to the bunker."

Nasir rolled his eyes and let out a soft laugh. "You worry too much, Mohammed. I'll be quick. I just need cigarettes. And besides, he is not here watching us now, is he?"

Mohammed knew arguing with his older brother was useless. If Nasir wanted to stop, he would stop. He had always had a mind of his own, always enjoyed thumbing his nose at those in power. "I—"

"Relax," Nasir said as he brought the truck to a jolting stop on the right side of the building. He gestured over his shoulder at the briefcase on the backseat. "Everything is fine. See?"

Mohammed followed his brother's gaze, his eyes lingering on the package. All the while, his right index finger caressed the trigger guard of the pistol he cradled in his lap. "I guess. But be fast."

"I'll be back before you know it." Nasir opened the door.

"Wait," Mohammed said, deciding to take advantage of the situation. "Get me some chocolate."

"Anything in particular?" Nasir asked.

Mohammed shook his head. "No. Whatever they have."

Nasir closed the door and turned for the store. As Nasir walked away, Mohammed performed a quick scan of his surroundings. His brother had parked them well away from other vehicles, orienting the truck so they had a three-hundred-sixty-degree view of anyone approaching. *At least he didn't forget to do that,* Mohammed consoled himself.

His thoughts turned to the evening and days ahead. Once he and Nasir delivered their package to Maksud's bunker and returned to Makhachkala, he had four days of free time. With tickets on the last flight to Tbilisi, he intended to spend the next ninety-six hours screwing the brains out of a pretty Georgian girl he had met on the internet a few months earlier.

18:59:04 MSK

Mohammed yawned and rubbed his eyes. He couldn't stop fantasizing about Oksana—how she would feel in his arms, taste on his lips. Soon enough, he told himself. He pushed the thoughts away and did another quick scan of the parking lot. *All clear.*

Nasir came out of the store. He carried two packs of cigarettes and two large green bottles of beer. His mischievous grin made Mohammed think, *Oh, no. What now?*

"My chocolate?" he asked as his brother climbed behind the wheel.

18:59:55 MSK

Nasir slapped his forehead.

18:59:57 MSK

"I forgot. I'll be right—"

19:00:00 MSK

Deep inside the package on the back seat of the GAZ, the trigger fashioned by Pytor came to life, unleashing an unstoppable chain reaction within the perfectly machined plutonium core. Within microseconds, the GAZ was gone, blasted to its constituent atoms by the new sun rising over Leninkent.

~ * * * ~

In nearby Makhachkala, the explosion shattered windows. The ground shook as if struck by an angry god. Citizens streamed into the streets to investigate, pointing in shocked awe at the dirty brown mushroom cloud towering above the town. From the courtyard of his compound, Maksud stared in mute horror as the cloud clawed its way into the stratosphere. Despite the terror of the moment, his thoughts were crystal clear, focused on one man: Magomed Gasanov. As his security force ushered him back into the dubious protective cover of his home, he began to formulate his plan for revenge.

THIRTY-FIVE

The White House
Office of the National Security Advisor

DOMINIC PLACED HIS TABLET ON the desk blotter and rested his elbows on the desk. Placing his head in his hands, he dug his thumbs into his temples and massaged in short, tight circles, trying in vain to drive the throbbing, skull-splitting pain away. Despite three Ibuprofens and a half-liter bottle of water an hour earlier, the headache that had been brewing in the back of his skull all morning showed no sign of easing. Straightening, he retrieved his tablet, blinked a few times to clear his vision, and resumed reading.

Noticing the time in the bottom corner of the screen, he couldn't help but wonder if Amanda's plane had landed. *It should have.* A faint smile tugged at the edges of his mouth as he recalled Kurt's reaction to the news.

Securing Amanda's release from the Canadian Security Intelligence Service had proved far more difficult than Dominic had ever imagined, pushing him to the brink of his ability to twist arms and lie with a smile. In the end, her release had hinged upon his ability to bluff his counterparts in Ottawa and his willingness to bend official policy to the point of breaking, including spinning a whopper of a threat about the United States withholding key aspects of intelligence sharing in the future. It had been touch and go for a few hours before his Canadian counterpart acceded to his demands.

Dominic had to admit he had enjoyed playing hardball with her captors. With all of the other disasters unfolding around him, it was satisfying to score a few points, to use the power of his office to do the right thing. In thc back of his mind, he did harbor concerns about what would happen if the new President ever discovered his subterfuge. He had no doubt he would be fired on the spot and driven out of government service in disgrace. But that would probably be the extent of it. And if that happened, would it really be so bad? Dominic was tired of government service. He didn't like the new President. Didn't like his policies. Didn't like the man. No, he decided. It wouldn't be such a bad thing.

Dominic's secure line rang once, a piercing, shrill sound that amplified the pain in his head tenfold. Dominic grasped the handset before it could ring again. At the same time, the mobile phone in his pocket buzzed to life, vibrating against his leg like a toothless chainsaw.

"Just a sec," he mumbled into the phone as he fished his mobile from his pocket. *What now?*

He brought his mobile up so he could read the screen.

PINNACLE/NUCFLASH
DAGESTAN, RUSSIAN REPUBLIC
UNAUTH/1B
YLD/15KT
AUTH/668BHA221C

The rest of the world fell away as Dominic stared openmouthed at his mobile phone. A PINNACLE/NUCLFLASH message, the rarest of the rare in emergency government communications, indicated a confirmed report of a nuclear event somewhere on the planet, an incident with the potential to ignite a large-scale nuclear conflict. According to the message, the explosion was unauthorized and had an estimated yield of fifteen kilotons. While small in terms of modern nuclear weapons, fifteen kilotons was still large enough to flatten a small city and kill tens of thousands of people.

Responding to a PINNACLE/NUCLFLASH was one of the scenarios for which Dominic had trained upon assuming the role of National Security Advisor, yet now that the unthinkable had become reality, all of the procedures and responses he had so carefully memorized escaped him.

His thoughts a confused jumble, Dominic took a deep breath and tried to steady his hands to keep a grip on the phone receiver that threatened to slip away. After a few more breaths, his composure returned.

"I'm on my way!" he barked as he got to his feet. He had to get to the Situation Room as fast as possible.

~ * * * ~

The President was on Dominic as soon as he

entered. “What the hell is going on in Dagestan?”

Dominic took a deep breath and tried to calm his raging pulse. He was more out of shape than he had realized. Or maybe it was the stress of the situation. “Sir, Dagestan is part of the Russian Federation. It was part of the former Soviet Union. There is no known nuclear presence there, and there never has been, according to my sources.” That was true, per the most recent briefing Dominic had received on the region, only three weeks prior.

The President moved to the head of the steel and glass conference table in the center of the room and placed his hands on the chair in front of him, one on top of each other. “Has this hit the news networks yet?”

Dominic checked his tablet, scanning the latest national intelligence media feed. “No, sir. Not yet.”

President Roswell licked his lips. “Good. This gives us some room to maneuver.” He nodded at a young staffer sitting at a computer in the corner. “I need a map.”

The video screen at the end of the table came to life, flooding the dim room with light. A high-resolution map of Dagestan appeared. A pulsing red circle surrounded a city on the eastern side of the country, on the far western edge of the Caspian Sea.

“Machala?” the President asked, butchering the pronunciation.

“Makhachkala,” Dominic corrected, earning him an annoyed scowl. Information on the former soviet state was flooding into his tablet, the result of a query he had launched in the elevator. “Population of a little over a half a million. Primarily Muslim. Their economy is agricultural with some medium-weight industry. They border Chechnya, and there was concern during the Chechen uprising they would be drawn into the conflict, but the threat never materialized."

The door opened, and the Chairman of the Joint Chiefs entered the room, followed by the director of the CIA, the Secretary of Homeland Security, and a handful of other cabinet officials and their support staff.

The President held up a finger to Dominic and turned his attention to the newcomers.

~ * * * ~

Dominic realized right away the meeting was going nowhere. Rather than engaging the problem, the President was looking for ways to avoid becoming entangled in events he didn't understand. Try as he might, Dominic couldn't help but compare the situation to the way President Cooper had handled the CIA affair and all of the other crises that had come his way during his tenure. While President Cooper would have immediately doled out the responsibility for dealing with the political, military, and intelligence activities to the various agency heads, President Roswell seemed intent upon shouldering the burden of the entire decision-making process himself, of assimilating every minute detail and owning the entire decision. That wasn't humanly possible; the crisis was too large. Being a member of the Russian Federation, Dagestan was a complete enigma to the United States. All they could do was guess, and guessing could be deadly in such a situation.

Dominic had sent several requests to his counterpart in Russia, but had received no response. His urgings to the President to pick up his phone and call the Russian president had so far gone ignored. For every minute that passed without contact, Dominic knew the chances of a catastrophic error of misunderstanding grew increasingly likely.

The LED in the corner of Dominic's tablet flashed twice, notifying him of a high-priority message. He tapped at his inbox, and the message expanded to fill his screen. It was from a contact within the National Reconnaissance Office, the agency responsible for launching and operating satellites for U.S. intelligence agencies. Based on the isotopes lofted into the atmosphere over Dagestan, the NRO estimated a ninety-three percent probability the material was from the same bomb that had vanished in Moscow several weeks earlier. But what made his breath catch in his throat was the news that the yield, estimated at twenty kilotons, was one-sixth the size of the missing warhead. That meant one of two things: either the warhead was a dud, or someone had split it into multiple devices, of which Dagestan was only the first target.

Helen was right.

Dominic went cold. It was the worst case scenario. Not only was a bomb missing, but whoever had it had the technical expertise to detonate it, or a part of it. He made a snap decision.

"Excuse me," he said, getting to his feet. "I have to make a call."

The conversation swirled around him, the other players barely noticing his abrupt departure. Once he reached the outside hall and closed the door behind him, he headed for the nearest Marine guard. "I need a private space to make a call."

"Sir. Down the hall. Second door on your right," the Marine responded.

"Thank you." Dominic took off down the hall, already dialing.

He found the room, knocked, and went inside when no one responded. Kurt was going to hate him for what he was about to ask, but Dominic had no other choice. The stakes were too high to wait.

THIRTY-SIX

Reagan National Airport Parking Garage

KURT COULDN'T TAKE HIS EYES off of Amanda as they strolled across the parking lot. "I can't believe you're here," he repeated for the fiftieth time, unable to wipe the grin from his face.

Amanda took his hand in hers and squeezed it. Kurt could tell from the smile stretching across her face that she felt the same way.

"Is this you?" she asked with a surprised grin as Kurt stopped in front of a glistening black Porsche 911 Carrera Four.

Kurt nodded, grinning.

"Can I drive?" Amanda asked with a gleam in her eye.

Kurt hadn't expected that. "Are you sure you're up to it?"

"I was in jail for a couple of days. It's not like I was being waterboarded in an Iraqi prison or something. I'm fine. Really."

Kurt tossed her the keys, and she snatched them out of the air. After seeing how well she had handled her Mini in London, he had no doubt she would be able to drive the Porsche.

His phone rang, and he checked the screen. “Hold on. It’s Dominic. Probably calling to make sure you arrived in one piece.”

“Are you still at the airport?” Dominic asked right away, his voice thick with urgency.

“Yeah. We’re about to get in my car.”

“Good. We don’t have time to talk. There’s been an explosion in the Russian Federation. Nuclear. I need you over there as soon as possible. We need eyes and ears on the ground, and Amanda knows the players.”

Kurt frowned. He leaned against the concrete pillar beside his car and rubbed his forehead.

“What is it?” Amanda whispered. Her smile had vanished, replaced by a furrowed brow and an almost imperceptible network of worry lines at the corners of her eyes.

Kurt shook his head and held up his finger. “I thought we were shut down,” he said to Dominic.

“You are,” Dominic replied, his frustration and exhaustion bleeding through the phone connection. “This is off the books. The President is dicking around, trying to figure out how to respond without becoming involved, and meanwhile, the Russians aren’t taking our calls. This could turn ugly really fast if they decide we were somehow involved. I need you two over there talking to people, working Amanda’s contacts, finding out whatever you can. I shouldn’t tell you this, but the bomb material in Dagestan contained the same isotopes as the Moscow device.”

“Helen was right,” Kurt whispered. He met Amanda’s eyes and mouthed, “Russia.”

“Exactly,” Dominic said.

“Shit,” Kurt muttered. “No support?”

“No. But don’t worry. I’ll work on it. Better to beg

for forgiveness later than ask permission and all that."

Kurt let out a defeated sigh. "Okay. Where do we start?"

"Start in Moscow. I'm chartering a jet at the General Aviation terminal. You won't be able to get into Dagestan. Not right away. The Russians are moving fast, trying to contain the news. They've instituted a total media blackout, but it won't last long. Once that happens, all hell will break loose."

"What do you want us to do?"

"Get in there. Find out what the Russians know. The yield doesn't match the records for the original warhead. I think there may be more bombs."

Kurt shivered at the possibility. "Okay. We're on it. We'll call from Moscow." He ended the call.

"Moscow?" Amanda asked with big eyes. "What do you mean, we'll call from Moscow?"

"You've got your passport, right?" Kurt asked.

"Yes. Well, a U.S. passport. The CSIS kept my Canadian papers."

Kurt took her by the arm and steered her back toward the airport. "Good enough. I've got money. We're going back to Russia."

"What?"

"There was an explosion in Dagestan, and according to Dominic, the isotope signature matches the Moscow bomb."

"And what does he expect us to do? I thought you said we were shut down."

Kurt sucked in his breath. "We are. We're not operating in any official capacity."

A mischievous smile crept onto Amanda's face. "As in, if we screw up, the government will disavow us? As in, we're on our own?"

"That's right," Kurt replied somberly. "Dominic said he would try to work things out on this end. He said the President is all jammed up, searching for the perfect solution, and it may take a while."

Amanda bowed her head, but only for a moment. When she raised it to meet his eyes, he could tell she had made her decision. She confirmed it when she asked, "What are we waiting for?"

They set out for the General Aviation terminal. Homecoming would have to wait.

~ * * * ~

In the White House basement, Dominic was barely able to contain himself as he turned the handle on the door to the Situation Room. Somewhere between receiving the call about the detonation and speaking with Kurt, his headache had miraculously vanished, and for the first time in hours, he was able to think clearly, to focus. He had already put in his request to the travel office for a private business jet. It would be ready by the time Kurt and Amanda reached the terminal.

As Dominic entered the room, the President turned his attention to him. "Thank you for rejoining us, Mr. Velasquez. Do you have something you'd like to share with the rest of us?"

Dominic couldn't believe the President was speaking to him like that, as if he were a child caught passing notes in class. Biting his lip, he swallowed his anger and plastered his most congenial smile on his face. "No, sir. Nothing at all."

The President stared at him for a moment in a futile attempt to assert his authority. Dominic let the man have his moment, confident the plan he had set into motion with Kurt and Amanda would prevail.

Finally, the President seemed to lose interest. "Good. In that case, I'd like to get back to the discussion. Where were we?"

Hurriedly taking his seat, Dominic picked up his tablet and began taking notes as the President droned on. He had some emails to send and a few more calls to make in the hours before Kurt and Amanda reached Russia. He needed to lay some groundwork in case things blew up in their faces.

It was going to be a long night.

THIRTY-SEVEN

Moscow

KURT GLANCED OVER HIS SHOULDER, staring through the rear window of the rented Volkswagen Passat. He searched for any signs that he and Amanda were being followed. "Are you sure we can trust him?"

"Absolutely," Amanda said as she checked the road and opened the driver's door. "Boris is something of an equal opportunity employee."

He followed her a moment later. "You mean..."

Amanda nodded. "I do. Both sides." The lights on the car flashed as Amanda locked it.

Kurt scanned the street once more and, not seeing anything suspicious, turned his attention back to Amanda.

"What are you looking for?" she asked.

Kurt gave an exaggerated shrug. "I don't know. I've just got a feeling..."

"Well, stop it. There's no one following us. Not yet. Come on." Taking his hand, she dragged him toward the lobby.

Amanda's plan, hatched thirty-seven thousand feet over the North Atlantic, had seemed sound with two vodka tonics in his belly and still riding high on the thrill of her return. But on the streets of Moscow, as they were about to enter the maw of the GRU, it seemed patently insane. Amanda's contact, a man she had collaborated with almost a decade earlier, was a longtime GRU officer, a Russian intelligence agent enmeshed deep within the machine of Russian state security. According to Amanda, Boris Carnov was, or had been, a reliable source of low- and medium-level information about GRU activities in the past. Whether the information he passed was state-sanctioned or born of his own initiative, she had never learned. Regardless, he still owed her for some information about an Israeli intelligence operation she had passed him a few years earlier.

An armored personnel carrier roared by on the street behind them, the sound echoing off the glass building they faced. The military presence in the capital was far greater than Kurt recalled from his last visit only a week before, not that he had spent much time observing the general state of the city. News of the explosion had breached the Russian media blackout while they were en route, and stock images of nuclear explosions and colorful maps of the region bordering the Caspian Sea had dominated the televisions tuned to twenty-four-hour news stations scattered throughout the airport. Despite the heightened state of alert, they had had no problems clearing immigration.

Cool air greeted them as they pushed through the heavy glass doors. The lobby exuded the spotless efficiency of a government intelligence facility, all black granite and stainless steel. A young man in a deep blue jacket sat behind an immaculate desk, a compact telephone headset snugged against his close-cropped brown hair. His eyes tracked Kurt and Amanda as they crossed the room with the intensity of a casino surveillance camera. The man barked something in rapid-fire Russian as they approached. Kurt looked to Amanda for guidance.

"Yes," she answered in English. "We have an appointment with Boris Carnov."

"You are American?" the receptionist asked, switching to English. It wasn't every day, Kurt figured, that an American walked into a GRU office building.

"Yes," Amanda said. "We are."

The man held out his hand. "Identification."

Amanda retrieved her passport from her pocket and motioned for Kurt to do the same. She placed both passports into the waiting hand.

Using a small laser scanner, the receptionist verified the authenticity of each passport. He kept one eye on his computer screen and one on Kurt and Amanda the entire time. Satisfied with the results, he placed the documents on the counter and nudged them across it. "Thank you, Ms. Carter, Mr. Vetter." He pointed at a cluster of plush leather chairs near the front door. "Please wait over there. Mr. Carnov will join you in a few minutes."

Amanda flashed him a smile. "Thank you."

"Thanks," Kurt added.

As they settled into their seats, Kurt leaned over and whispered, "What was that about?"

Amanda's face grew hard, and she rolled her eyes toward the ceiling suggestively.

Kurt got the message. *We're being watched.* Somewhere inside the building, maybe on the other side of the flush metal door behind the desk, a camera system was surely recording every movement for later analysis. He closed his mouth and lifted his right leg to cross it over his left at the knee.

Two minutes later, an unmarked door beside the elevator snapped open. A giant of a man with a bushy shock of gray hair emerged, stopping momentarily to ensure the door closed tightly behind him. He turned around, and upon seeing Amanda, his face split into a joyous grin. He strode quickly across the room, spreading his arms as he approached.

"Here we go," Amanda whispered. She stood and took a step forward to greet the man.

"Amanda!" Boris exclaimed. "Welcome back to Moscow!" They exchanged cheek kisses, and then Boris held her at arm's length, looking her up and down, inspecting every inch of her. "You look better than I remember."

"Thanks, Boris. You, too," Amanda said, blushing. "A little grayer on the top, but otherwise you haven't changed a bit."

She gestured at Kurt. "Boris, this is my colleague, Mr. Vetter."

"Hello." Kurt extended his hand. Boris shook it, and Kurt couldn't help but notice the steely strength in his grip. "It's nice to meet you. Amanda has told me a lot about you."

Boris leered at Amanda. "I hope nothing bad."

Kurt forced a laugh. "I don't think so."

"Come," Boris said, setting off toward the front door. "There's a wonderful cafe down the street, next to the university. It just opened."

"Roll with it," Amanda whispered to Kurt as she fell in behind Boris.

Ten minutes later, Kurt found himself ensconced in a deep booth in the rear of Boris's favorite coffee shop. He struggled to breathe through the viscous haze of cigarette and marijuana smoke.

"I love this place," Boris gushed. "It is close to both

my office and the university. Many young people come here, many young girls." He gave a lecherous nod at a tattooed blonde sitting on a stool near the door. "It provides a nice distraction from my office." He punctuated his words with a deep belly laugh.

Amanda laughed along with him. "You never change, do you?"

Boris kept the smile on his face, but his voice grew serious. "We can speak here, but not for long. I am not the only one who comes for the sights." He cast a furtive glance around the room, as though he were double-checking his earlier assessment. "Tell me, what brings you to Moscow?"

Amanda's knee brushed against Kurt's under the table, pressed for a moment, and then moved away. "We're looking for someone..."

Boris sipped his coffee. "And who might this *someone* be?"

"Someone in your organization, the person running the intelligence side of the Dagestan investigation."

Boris choked on his drink, spraying a few drops of coffee on the table. He dabbed at them with his napkin. "Alexander Yolkin? What do you want with him?"

Kurt made a mental note of the name.

Amanda tilted her head in a show of exasperation. "Let's just say there is not a good flow of information between our governments at the moment."

Boris nodded. "Yes. I know this."

Amanda continued. "We have information that may help Mr. Yolkin. And we believe he may have information useful to us."

Boris looked down at his coffee cup. He traced his thumb around the rim of the cup. "Yolkin is... how do you say? Old school? He is not a man to be trifled with."

"I expected nothing less," Amanda said. "Still, we need to speak with him."

Boris raised an eyebrow, but didn't ask why. Kurt crossed his fingers under the table, hoping the ruse would work.

After an interminable moment of consideration, Boris gave a faint nod. "Okay. I can get you to Yolkin. But you have to promise," he said, reaching across the table to touch the back of Amanda's hand, "to be very careful. He is a dog. Corner him, and he will bite."

Amanda gave Boris's hand a pat. "I'll be careful. I promise."

"And you, Mr. Vetter?" Boris shifted his gaze to Kurt. "You would be well served to follow the lead of your colleague."

Kurt gave him a slight nod. "Of course."

They spent the next few minutes discussing how to get close to Yolkin, covering at great lengths where he worked, his typical schedule, the car he drove, even where he lived. Boris's unease was obvious. Each bit of information Amanda extracted made the man appear a little more frazzled, as if he were drifting well outside of his comfort zone.

Finally, Boris lifted his sleeve and checked his watch. "I have to get back to my office. I have a meeting in ten minutes." He started to slide from the booth, but Amanda stopped him with a hand on his wrist.

"Thank you," she said, locking the older man in her gaze. "You may have saved a lot of lives today."

Boris's mouth opened and closed as if he wanted to say something else, but he held his tongue. Instead, he leaned in for a final kiss from Amanda. A moment later he was gone, swallowed by the crowds near the door.

"Did you get that?" Amanda asked.

Kurt was busy scribbling the last few details provided by Boris on the back of a napkin. "Yep. Got it."

"Good. That wasn't too bad now, was it?"

Kurt thought about it for a moment. "No. Actually, it was almost too easy. I'm waiting for the next shoe to drop."

Amanda chuckled and pulled a fistful of rubles from her pocket. She dumped enough to cover the coffee and a small tip onto the table. Sliding toward the edge of the booth, she said, "Let's get out of here."

Kurt didn't put up an argument.

THIRTY-EIGHT

Washington
The White House

"YOU DID *WHAT*?"

DOMINIC CLENCHED his teeth and forced himself to hold the President's gaze, even though he wanted to break eye contact with every fiber of his being. He had known the President would be angry when he informed him of his insubordination, but he had not been prepared for the barely contained fury before him.

"Sir, I understand you are upset with my actions. You have every right to be. However, that doesn't change the fact that the intelligence provided by Ms. Bartholomew was correct, and that what you... what *we* hoped was a Russian problem has now become ours as well. I had a strong sense the situation was worse than it appeared on the surface, so I sent Mr. Vetter and Ms. Carter to Moscow to see if they could work the back channels and find out what the Russians were doing."

The President put his head in his hands and stared at the surface of his desk. His knuckles turned white as he pressed his fingertips into his scalp, digging into his wavy gray hair as if kneading dough. He dropped his hands and looked up at Dom. "You realize what this means, don't you?"

Dominic gave a tentative nod. "Yes, sir. I'm well aware of the repercussions."

The President blew out a hard breath. "I told you that operation was shut down, that I wanted to work this through established government agencies, yet you ignored me, went behind my back, and did the exact opposite. What in the hell were you thinking? That I wouldn't find out? That those two could just drop into Moscow like James Bond and solve all of our problems, get the Russians to start talking to us? This isn't the movies, Dominic. It doesn't work that way!" The President screamed the final words, all semblance of control abandoned.

"No, sir," Dominic said. "It's not that simp—"

"Shut up! I'm not done!" The President slammed his open palm on the desk with an earsplitting *CRACK*. "We have people for this sort of thing, experts in State, CIA, and even the NSA, people who know what the fuck they're doing. The last thing we need right now is a bunch of cowboys running around Moscow, throwing gas on this fire."

"Sir, the last thing Kurt and Amanda are is amateur. They can handle themselves, and I made it very clear to them that they do not represent the U.S. government. They're on their own."

The President cocked his head. "On their own? What do you mean?"

Sensing an opening to defuse the President's fury, Dominic pressed on. "They're operating as private citizens... because I asked them as a personal favor."

The President considered that for a moment, and his mouth twisted into a devious smile. “So if they were to get killed or captured, I... *we* don’t have to bail them out?”

So that’s what this is about. “Exactly. We have complete deniability. Kurt and Amanda are simple tourists who happen to know a few people in the Russian government.”

The President leaned back, the chair creaking under his weight. He fished a pack of Marlboros from his suit jacket, shook one out, and lit it with a silver Zippo. He blew a tight stream of smoke at the ceiling. Dominic watched and waited, well aware the moment was the crux of the conversation, the point at which the President either kicked him out on his ass or gave him a chance to run the operation to its natural conclusion, to redeem himself.

“I want your resignation on my desk by midnight,” the President said. “If, and this is a big if, your people manage to pull this off, we’ll forget we ever had this conversation. But make no mistake, if they fuck up, you’re out on your ass, and I’ll do my damnedest to make sure you never work in this town again.” His eyes narrowed. “Do you understand me? You won’t be able to get a job dusting Lincoln’s nuts by the time I’m done with you.”

Dominic was perfectly clear. Everything, the entire investigation into the explosion in Dagestan, the disposition of the stolen bomb, and last, but not least, his career, was on the line. Kurt and Amanda had to deliver, or it was all over.

“Yes, sir,” he said with far more conviction than he felt.

The President glared at him, his eyes blazing with contempt. “Now, get the hell out of my office. Find something or else start packing.”

Without another word, Dominic got to his feet. Giving the President a quick nod, he turned and strode for the door.

As he reached the hall, he exhaled an enormous sigh of relief. The hard part was done. The weight of the world seemed to have lifted away, replaced by a calming sense of acceptance. He set off for his office at a brisk stride, intent on doing everything in his power and then some to ensure he delivered.

THIRTY-NINE

Moscow, Russia

AMANDA GRABBED KURT'S WRIST, SQUEEZING so hard it hurt. She pointed and hissed, "That's him."

Kurt squinted through the afternoon sun's glare on the windshield, trying to make out the man she had indicated. He couldn't be a hundred percent certain, but the man sure seemed to match Boris's description, down to the thin fringe of wispy hair encircling his head and the way he waddled down the street, as if he had something stuck deep inside his ass. A training injury from his early days in the GRU, Boris had said, both ankles broken and set improperly by a Soviet Army field doctor. How Boris knew that, Kurt had been afraid to ask.

"Are you ready?" he asked.

Amanda nodded and opened the glove box to withdraw a scuffed and scratched pistol that had seen far better days. She had purchased the gun, a Tokarev TT, just off the A-104, on their way into the city from the airport. According to the man who had taken

Amanda's folded stack of twenties, it worked like new. Kurt had his doubts, but after a quick once-over, Amanda had declared it suitable.

Kurt had the wheel. Amanda sat in the front passenger seat, her hand poised on the door latch. The streets glistened a liquid black, soaked by an intense rainsquall a few minutes earlier. Kurt inhaled deeply through his cracked window, drawing the lingering fresh ozone scent into his nostrils. They had both been worried that the rain would interfere with Yolkin's regular Wednesday afternoon appointment with his mistress, but the man was determined. He had emerged from his office exactly on schedule, carrying a short black umbrella tucked under his arm, glanced at the sky, and then set off down the street.

According to Boris, Yolkin kept his car in an underground garage a half-block from his office. Unlike the old days of the Soviet Union, Yolkin's position didn't warrant a driver, so he was forced to walk to his car. This was their window, Kurt had decided, the moment at which they would make their move. Complicating matters, however, was their proximity to Yolkin's office. If they acted too soon, there was a good chance they would find themselves surrounded by the Russian police force, or worse, GRU thugs. That was the last thing either of them wanted. On the other hand, if they waited too long, Yolkin would reach the safety of the garage, and their opportunity would be lost.

Kurt despised operating under such tight constraints, but according to Boris, it was their best, and maybe only, shot. Yolkin's defenses would be down since he was focused on his mistress. Snatching him from the street was their only choice. If they could pull it off and get him into the car, they could interrogate him at their leisure.

"Go," Amanda said as Yolkin strolled by their position. "Stay a length behind him until we reach the corner." The corner was their point of no return, they had agreed, the moment at which they had to grab Yolkin, or else abandon the hunt and start over.

A motorcycle buzzed by on Kurt's left, narrowly missing the driver's side mirror. The bike screamed like an angry insect, and then it was gone, swallowed by the constant traffic.

Kurt kept one eye on Yolkin and the other on the traffic as he crept along, trying not to be swept away by the incessant flow, while at the same time leaving room for a quick escape.

One car length.

Two.

Three.

A bell chimed softly, announcing an opened door. Kurt realized Amanda was out of the car, weaving between the bumpers of two parked vehicles, moving into position a few feet behind Yolkin. He gave the car a little gas, moving in front of them, then tapped the brakes. He punched the button to turn on his emergency flashers and gripped the wheel tightly while reciting a quick prayer. A furtive glance over his shoulder confirmed no one was coming to Yolkin's aid. Not yet.

Amanda moved like a cheetah stalking an unsuspecting gazelle, sidling up behind Yolkin in two quick steps and digging the barrel of her pistol into his lower back. Leaning into his ear, she whispered something Kurt hoped he would never himself hear, and then put an arm on the older man's elbow, turning him in Kurt's direction.

A moment later, she hauled open the front door and shoved the aging spy into the passenger seat. Yolkin barked a protest in guttural Russian—

expletives, Kurt guessed—and shot Kurt an indignant, furious glare. Kurt pursed his lips and shook his head.

Then, the rear door slammed, and Amanda slapped her palm on his headrest. “Drive!”

Yolkin twisted in his seat to face Amanda. He said something else in Russian, but stopped with his mouth open when Amanda said, “Speak English.”

“Americans. I should have known,” Yolkin said, his voice dripping with disgust. “Do you have any idea who I am?”

“We do,” Amanda replied.

Yolkin’s face boiled with unconstrained rage. “I demand you stop immediately.” His right hand moved toward his breast pocket.

Amanda cocked her pistol. “Don’t.”

Yolkin lifted his hand slowly away from his chest. “It is only my telephone. I am not armed.”

Keeping her gun trained on him, Amanda reached over the seat and into his breast pocket. She plucked out a slim mobile phone and held it up in front of his face. “This?”

Yolkin nodded.

Amanda took the device and placed it on the seat beside her.

“What do you want?” Yolkin asked.

A break in the traffic appeared, and Kurt accelerated. “When do I turn?”

“Left, two streets up,” Amanda said. “Then take your first right.”

Kurt followed her directions without question, and a minute later, he turned off the main road into a narrow parking lot fronting an abandoned warehouse.

“Go around back,” Amanda ordered, gesturing at an alley entrance with her gun. Kurt did.

The building appeared much larger from the rear, stretching at least a full city block. Dilapidated loading docks punctuated the facade every few hundred feet, jutting out like forgotten piers in an ocean of cracked concrete. Kurt brought the car to a stop and slipped the transmission into neutral. He left the engine running, one hand covering the gear shift and his left foot resting above the clutch pedal in case they had to move fast.

"Why are we stopping?" Yolkin demanded. Kurt noticed what he thought was a glimmer of uncertainty in the man's eyes, and he spotted a faint bead of perspiration growing on his forehead.

"You Americans are so foolish," the Russian said, the absolute calm of his voice dashing Kurt's hopes. "You think you can get away with this? Here? In Moscow? You must know my colleagues are looking for me at this very moment."

Kurt laughed. "I don't think so. I'm pretty sure everyone in your office assumes you're off screwing your mistress." He made a show of checking his watch. "I figure we have at least an hour or two before anyone notices you haven't returned."

Yolkin scowled at Kurt and shifted in his seat, turning so he could see Amanda as well.

"Look," Kurt said. "It's important we talk. You have information we need, information beneficial to both of our nations. We were forced to improvise."

"Improvise?" Yolkin emitted a grating laugh. "Is that what you call this?"

Kurt exchanged a sidelong glance with Amanda. He sensed the conversation was getting away from him, that Yolkin was trying to go on the offensive. He had to steer the discussion back on track. "It's complicated. We know about the Chechen."

Yolkin raised an eyebrow, and the anger drained from his face, replaced by wary suspicion. He sat up straighter in his seat. "I'm listening."

Thunder rumbled outside, and a steady rain began to fall, quickly growing from a light sprinkle to a raging downpour, building to a staccato roar on the roof of the Passat.

"We know he double-crossed our CIA people, that he took the real bomb. What we don't know is how he did it and who he was working with."

"And why should I tell you?" Yolkin asked.

Amanda shifted her gaze to her gun and then back to Yolkin.

Yolkin locked eyes with her. He sighed. "Very well. I can't speak to the motivations behind the plot. However, I can confirm the Chechen has been killed, and the nuclear material is once again under our control."

"Killed?" Kurt asked, incredulous.

Yolkin's gaze shifted from Amanda's gun back to Kurt. "A little over an hour ago. Outside of Grozny."

The rain tapered off, and the interior of the car brightened as the sun peeked through the clouds.

"How?" Amanda asked.

Yolkin turned back to her. "It seems our Chechen friend underestimated one of his former allies in Dagestan. Our current theory is that the device in Leninkent was Gasanov's attempt to eliminate the Dagestani, and at the same time, to announce to the world he possessed the weapons—"

"That doesn't make sense," Kurt insisted, rubbing his chin. "Why use a nuke to kill a rival? There have to be better uses for such a device."

Yolkin shrugged. "As I said, our investigation is still underway."

"But you have the remaining plutonium?" Amanda asked.

"We do."

Kurt chewed on Yolkin's information for a moment,

trying to fit the pieces together in his head. It sounded too simple. Yolkin was leaving something out, something critical. "What about—"

"Excuse me," Yolkin interrupted, reaching into the foot well and scratching vigorously at his lower leg.

Kurt looked to Amanda, trying to read her expression, to see if she believed Yolkin's story. Then, out of the corner of his eye, he caught a glint of metal. "Watch out! He's got a gun!"

Amanda swiveled her aim until her weapon brushed Yolkin's back. "Drop it!"

Faster than Kurt thought possible for such an old man, Yolkin twisted his body away from Amanda's pistol and reared up holding a slim weapon of his own. He pointed it at Kurt's face.

The weapon must have been strapped to his ankle, Kurt realized with a sickening certainty. Despite the diminutive size, he knew full well that, in such close quarters, the gun would be deadly.

Yolkin held out his free hand. "Our conversation is over. I'd like my phone back."

Amanda moved to reach for it, but Kurt cut her off. "Wait! I have one more question."

"I think we should do what he says," Amanda said, her eyes boring into him.

Kurt shook his head, then fixed his gaze on Yolkin. He tried to ignore the sense of impending doom in his gut. "Tell me about Viktor Durov." For the briefest of moments, he swore he saw recognition in Yolkin's eyes, but as soon as it was there, it was gone, replaced by a stubborn indignation.

"I don't know anyone by that name," Yolkin growled. "Now, if you'll return my phone—"

Kurt considered the Russian's response. He knew Yolkin was lying, knew it like he knew the sky was blue. That made Yolkin that much more dangerous.

He sighed. The conversation was indeed over. “Give him his phone.”

Amanda handed over the device, and Yolkin deposited it into his breast pocket.

“I’m getting out now,” Yolkin announced, reaching for the door release. “I regret to say this has not been a pleasure.”

Once Yolkin was out, he slammed the door and took a few steps back. He reached into his breast pocket, pulled his phone, then started to dial.

“Oh shit,” Amanda said as she squeezed into the front seat. “Go! He’s calling in backup! The embassy! Now!”

Kurt threw the car into gear and popped the clutch. They shot forward, and as he watched in the rearview mirror, he saw Yolkin gesturing wildly at the air, screaming into his phone. It was only a matter of minutes before the might of the Russian security forces descended upon them.

FORTY

Moscow, Russia
City Center

KURT TORE THROUGH THE CENTER of Moscow, weaving in and out of traffic so fast that the other cars seemed to be standing still. At Amanda's urging, he blew through every red light he encountered, bracing for impact each time, yet miraculously coming out unscathed on the other side.

Still, the Russian security forces were gaining, and Kurt knew they couldn't outrun a radio. It was only a matter of time before a blockade appeared in front of them, and the ride would be over.

"Kurt! Watch out!" Amanda threw up her arms to cover her face and shrank back into her seat.

Kurt glanced up just in time to see a tractor-trailer lumbering toward their right front quarter-panel, moments away from a direct collision. He jammed his foot down on the brake and wrenched the wheel to the left. Once he felt the car beginning to swing around, he gunned the engine and, against all odds, they squeaked past the enormous vehicle and onto an empty side street.

"Shit," he muttered. He wiped the sweat from his forehead. "That was too—"

"Turn!" Amanda insisted, pointing at a larger cross street full of slow-moving traffic. "That's Bolshoy Deviatinsky Pereulok; the embassy is only a few blocks away."

"Are you sure?"

"Just do it!"

In the rearview mirror, Kurt saw a blizzard of flashing lights behind them, all ignoring the direction of the road. He wrenched the wheel to the right. The tires of the Volkswagen screamed in protest as they tore around the corner, nearly flattening an old man in the middle of the crosswalk.

To Kurt's relief, he found they were once again traveling with the flow of traffic. In the distance, he recognized the unmistakable facade of the old embassy building, the ornate yellow structure glittering in the afternoon sun like a beacon in a storm. The new embassy compound, less visible from the road, was next door. They were almost home. According to Amanda, Boris was supposed to have called in an anonymous tip, to prepare the embassy staff for their imminent arrival.

"What's that?" Kurt asked, leaning forward and squinting. The traffic ahead, near the embassy, was slowing to a crawl. A group of men in uniforms stood in the road, facing in their direction. One spoke into a radio.

"What do I do? What do I do?" Panic gripped him. He could *see* the embassy, goddamn it; it was just down the street. He wasn't about to go this far only to give up. He knew what he had to do before Amanda confirmed it.

"Run it," she said.

Kurt tightened his grip on the steering wheel, exhaled, and jammed the accelerator to the floor. They quickly closed on the roadblock, the stopped traffic filling his view, their options falling away with each passing second. He cut the wheel violently, veering away from the stopped traffic and bumping over a low curb and onto a sidewalk running parallel to the road. Solid metal lampposts flashed by on his left, high stone walls on the right. The space was barely large enough to permit their passage. Barely, but enough.

Over the roar of the engine, Kurt heard a faint *pop, pop, pop,* and a split-second later, the windshield exploded into his lap, showering him with dime-sized chunks of glistening safety glass. He felt a sting on his forehead and reached up to wipe at it. His fingers came away covered with blood. He blinked as blood flowed into his left eye, partially obstructing his vision.

They shot past the edge of the roadblock and found the street ahead clear of vehicles. But there was a new problem; the sidewalk came to an end a few hundred yards ahead, a few seconds at most, where the wall surrounding the U.S. embassy began. Kurt had no choice. He spun the wheel hard to the left, sending them bouncing back over the curb, narrowly missing one of the lampposts, and back onto Bolshoy Deviatinsky Pereulok.

Amanda cried out as the impact sent her careening into the roof. The Passat roared as if in agony, and steam erupted from under the hood, flowing up and into the passenger compartment as they lurched to a broken stop, less than fifty yards from the Embassy gate.

Kurt stole a glance in the mirror, and his heart almost stopped. Strobe lights filled the road as police and military vehicles descended on them in droves. In the other direction, beyond the embassy gates, he saw the same thing. They were out of time.

"Out of the car!" he ordered. "Now!"

Amanda tumbled out of view, and a second later, she was sprinting ahead, racing toward the gate. Kurt took off at a dead run, unable to catch up, but maintaining her pace.

Looking ahead at the gate, he saw they had an audience. The normal contingent of Marines guarding the gate had been reinforced and numbered at least a dozen, all maintaining position at the extreme edge of the Embassy property, technically on U.S. soil.

"Almost there..." he gasped, and put on a last burst of speed.

"Passport!" Amanda barked, reaching into her pants pocket and pulling out the small blue folder. She flipped it open as she ran, screaming, "U.S. Citizen! U.S. Citizen!" over and over.

Kurt slapped his right leg pocket, searching for his own identification. He couldn't remember where he had stashed it. His heart fluttered for a split second when he couldn't find it. Then, he tried his left leg and felt the familiar outline. Pulling it out, he held it in front of him and joined Amanda in her chorus of "U.S. Citizen!"

The Marines at the gate, stony-faced and forming an impenetrable barrier of flesh and steel until that moment, parted to allow them through, and then closed the gap behind them as if it had never existed.

Kurt came to a stumbling stop as he passed the last Marine. Bending over with his hands on his knees, he struggled to catch his breath. His stomach heaved, and for a moment, he thought he was going to vomit. The feeling passed as quickly as it had come on, and when he looked over at Amanda, he saw that she, too, was bent over, trying to catch her breath.

Straightening, he made his way to her.
They had made it. They were safe.
At last.

FORTY-ONE

06:05 EDT
Cumberland Federal Penitentiary
Cumberland, Maryland

VIKTOR DUROV PAUSED AT THE entrance to the prison yard, scanning his new surroundings for the first time. To his immediate left, a group of tattooed men worked methodically with a rusty collection of iron weights, their grunts and groans echoing off the concrete walls of the yard like wild animals in a cage. Directly in front of him, a small cluster of men loitered at a pair of weather-beaten picnic tables, their voices barely a murmur. Viktor's gaze moved on, taking in several more groups of men as well as a few loners. Seeing nothing that concerned him, he entered the yard.

His transfer to the medium security prison in Western Maryland had happened in the dead of night four days earlier. There had been no warning, no explanation. His attorney, as far as he could tell, had not yet caught up with him. The lack of information concerning his disposition was starting to wear on him. The guards were useless, stony-faced automatons that cared only about their orders. His requests to use the telephone had so far fallen on deaf ears.

Turning to his right, Viktor followed the wall toward a lone man smoking beside a leafless tree. As he approached, the man shook a cigarette out of his pack and held it out, along with a pack of matches.

"Morning," the man said, his voice barely audible.

Viktor grunted and took the proffered cigarette. He lit up, drawing the cool smoke deep into his lungs. The other man inhabited the cell across from his own and had been Viktor's only contact since his arrival. While he didn't know the man well enough to trust him, he also didn't fear him. Viktor smoked in silence, his attention focused on a trio of wispy clouds scudding by on the horizon. The other man said nothing, focusing on his own cigarette as if it were the last smoke in the world.

Viktor tensed when he heard the sound of footsteps behind him. His neighbor's eyes grew wide, and the guy took a sudden lurching step backward, spinning away from Viktor. The sounds of the men at the weights had vanished, Viktor realized. He turned, prepared to fight, and found himself face to face with a man about his height, only twenty pounds heavier. The man's eyes blazed as if he were riding high on meth.

Viktor held up his palms. "I don't want any trouble—"

"This is from Yolkin," the bald man growled, lunging deep into Viktor's personal space. Before Viktor could process the words, a sharp pain erupted deep in his belly, spiking quickly into a searing bolt of agony encompassing his entire torso. A sudden sensation of warmth drenched his legs. *My blood*, he realized absently. Looking down, Viktor watched in horror as the bald man withdrew a five-inch homemade knife from his stomach, wiped the rusty blade on his shirt, and then dropped it to the ground with a clatter.

Casting a nonchalant glance over his shoulder, the man turned and strode away, heading in the general direction of the picnic tables in the middle of the yard.

Viktor tried to call out, but his mouth filled with blood. He choked and fell to his knees. Clutching the gash in his midsection, he saw his life unspooling before his eyes. Darkness swooped in from the periphery of his vision, stealing bits and pieces of his existence, until, finally, everything went black.

~ * * * ~

14:05 EDT
The White House
Office of the National Security Advisor

"Thank you," Dominic said as his assistant placed a silver tray containing a brushed-steel carafe of coffee and three delicate china cups on the small wooden table.

"Yes, thank you," Amanda echoed.

Dominic's assistant acknowledged them with a demure nod, then turned and left the room.

As soon as the door closed, Kurt picked up the carafe and filled their cups. He waited for the others to prepare their coffee; sugar and cream for Dominic and a single green and white packet of Truvia for Amanda. Kurt took his black. He blew into his cup and took a tentative sip, taking care not to burn his lips on the scalding liquid. It was good. White House coffee, he had learned, was *always* good.

Dominic took a sip, then cradled his cup in his hands. "Thanks for coming in today. This won't take long."

Kurt and Amanda exchanged a glance. On the drive in from Annapolis, they had debated long and hard about the subject of the meeting. Kurt was convinced Dominic was going to disband their nascent organization and send Darlene back to the NSA, him back to the CIA, and Amanda God-knew-where. Amanda, on the other hand, was certain Dominic had good news.

They had returned from Russia only two days before. The fallout from their actions in Moscow was still being felt on both sides of the Atlantic, although in Kurt's opinion, the Russians were being oddly silent. He knew better than to ask questions, though. Someone had pulled some major strings to extricate him and Amanda from the embassy in one piece. He supposed it was the President. He was the only one with that type of power, after all. If that were the case, though, it would represent a complete change of heart, one Kurt wasn't sure he believed possible given what he knew about the man.

Darlene had been ecstatic to see Kurt and Amanda back in the States in one piece. In their absence, she had continued working to establish the connection between Durov and the SEWS attack and to find any information that might assist them. Once she had received word of Yolkin's identity, and knew where to search, it had been a simple matter for her to make the final connection between the Durovs and their controllers. The evidence, extracted from an almost untraceable series of financial transactions and international telephone calls spanning decades, was unassailable, and Kurt was confident it had played a key role in their unmolested departure from Russian soil. It would have been too embarrassing for the Russian government if the truth came out, for the world to know an element of their government had launched a covert attack on the United States. That was his best guess, at least. According to Darlene, she had passed her findings up the chain of command and had never heard another word until Dominic called back with news of their imminent return.

"Durov is dead," Dominic announced, as if commenting on the weather. "He was stabbed to death this morning at Cumberland Federal Penitentiary. No one saw the attack, of course."

Kurt almost spilled his coffee at this news. "Dead? Are you serious?"

Dominic dabbed at his mouth with a linen napkin. "I'm afraid so."

"That was fast," Amanda said.

Dominic arched an eyebrow. "What do you mean?"

Amanda set her coffee on the table and took a breath. "I believe the Russians are trying to cover their tracks. Durov. Yolkin. Gasanov. All of it. The attack on the SEWS was a failed experiment, an attempt to extend their reach. Gasanov and his bombs, well, that was an unfortunate coincidence for the Russians. Without that distraction, their plan may have actually worked."

Kurt nodded, pleased to hear her assessment so closely mirrored his own. Still, something in her comment had triggered an almost-forgotten memory, a reminder of how one of Yolkin's statements had made him wonder if he was leaving something out. It all made sense. Whether Yolkin was behind the attack on the Strategic Early Warning System, or if he only knew of its existence secondhand, he must have realized they would eventually put the pieces together. That explained his motivation for acting so brashly.

Dominic crossed his legs. "I concur, although I'm sure there will be more fallout once the dust settles. Right now, I suspect there's a major housecleaning going on in the Russian government."

"No doubt," Amanda said. "I wouldn't want to be there right now."

"Do you think they really thought they could get away with it?" Kurt asked.

Dominic shrugged. "Who knows? You'd be surprised at some of the hare-brained schemes people come up with in this business."

Kurt wasn't satisfied with the answer, but he realized Dominic didn't know much more than he did.

Dominic regarded them for a moment. "And now for some good news. I had a meeting with President Roswell this morning. After your most recent success in Russia, he's finally come around to seeing the benefit of our arrangement. He wants to make it permanent, even to increase your funding. Now, it's just a matter of deciding what we want to do with it."

Amanda patted Kurt's arm. "See? I told you."

Kurt felt a keen sense of relief at the news, mixed with a nagging feeling of dread. They were three for three. How long could that last? In his mind, their success was due as much to luck as skill. He had been in the right place at the right time, and everything had worked out. What would happen the next time, when the odds weren't in his favor? When he found himself in over his head once again, and there was no one there to show him the way forward?

"That's great news," he said with a forced smile. "Darlene and the rest of the staff will be happy to hear they still have jobs."

Dominic laughed at this. "Oh, you have nothing to

worry about on that front. In fact, I've already got your first official assignment."

"First assignment?" Kurt and Amanda said in unison.

"Yep," Dominic said, pulling out a manila folder from his desk drawer and opening it. "What do you know about China?"

ABOUT THE AUTHOR

William Esmont lives in Southern Arizona with his wife, their three dogs, and one cat. *Pressed* is his fourth novel, and the second in the *Reluctant Hero* series. He is also working on a horror series, *Elements of the Undead*. The first book in this collection, *Fire*, was released in May 2011, and he released a novelette, *Air*, in September of 2011. The next installment is due in the summer of 2012.

If you enjoyed this story, please take a moment to leave a positive review. Good reviews help sell stories, which in turn, allows William to write more.

If you'd like to contact William, you can reach him thorough the following channels:

Email: William.Esmont@gmail.com
Web: www.WilliamEsmont.com
Twitter: @WilliamEsmont
Facebook: tinyurl.com/WilliamEsmont-Facebook

11068484R00152

Made in the USA
Charleston, SC
28 January 2012